ALSO BY NEIL McGAUGHEY

The Best Money Murder Can Buy

And Then There Were Ten

Otherwise Known As Murder

A CORPSE BY ANY OTHER NAME

A Stokes Moran Mystery

NEIL McGAUGHEY

Scribner

SCRIBNER
1230 Avenue of the Americas
New York, NY 10020

This book is a work of fiction. Names, characters, places, and
incidents either are products of the author's imagination or are used
fictitiously. Any resemblance to actual events or locales or persons,
living or dead, is entirely coincidental.

Text set in Bodoni Book

Manufactured in the United States of America

1 3 5 7 9 10 8 6 4 2

Library of Congress Cataloging-in-Publication Data
McGaughey, Neil.
A corpse by any other name: a Stokes Moran mustery/
Neil McGaughey.
p.   cm.
I. Title.
PS3563.C36372C67   1998
813'.54—dc21   97–37234
CIP
ISBN-10: 1-4165-7511-1
ISBN-13: 978-1-4165-7511-5

For my parents
Noel and Lula McGaughey
Thicker than blood

ACKNOWLEDGMENTS

I would like to express grateful and heartfelt thanks to the following individuals:

To the early readers of this manuscript—Nolan and Nancy Minton, Sue Hathorn, Lynn Clark, Jane Lee, Mark Smith and Shirley Tipton, and Bill and Julie Kehoe;

To my mystery writer friends Nevada Barr, D. J. Donaldson, Sophie Dunbar, and Earline Fowler;

To my agent Martha Kaplan;

To my Scribner editor Susanne Kirk;

To my former *Clarion-Ledger* editor Orley Hood; and

To Don and Tracey.

Finally, I cannot sufficiently express my appreciation to Wanda Edge of Jacksonville, Florida, who presented me with the most precious gift of my life—a two-year-old Irish setter named CeeCee.

A **CORPSE** BY ANY OTHER NAME

CHAPTER **ONE**

*"Readers
looking for a serious hard-boiled novel
better skirt a wide detour
around this one
lest its contagious good humor
and lighthearted style
cause them severe bodily harm."*

—Stokes Moran,
on Rita Mae Brown's *Murder at Monticello*

" *A* "

Is for Alibi, "B" Is for Burglar, "C" Is for Corpse . . .
"S" Is for Stupid?

Have you ever played the game? The Grafton Game? I
know a number of mystery fans, including myself, who do.

But if you're not a player, then all I can say for you is *"D"
Is for Deadbeat.* Or *"W" Is for Wimp.*

The rules of the game are simple. You merely try to out-
guess author Sue Grafton on her alphabet choices for Kinsey
Millhone's future adventures. Several years ago, as a mental
exercise during a power blackout, I compiled a list by can-
dlelight, all the way from *G* (you see, I came late to the party)
to *Z*. Not wanting to limit myself to just one entry per letter, I
jotted down both serious and comic alternatives for each,
even revising my selections as the years have passed.

And, from time to time, I will pull out the list and see how I'm doing. The good news: I've occasionally hit the target right on the mark—*"H" Is for Homicide* and *"K" Is for Killer* are two of my notable successes. But more times than not, I've missed badly—*"G" Is for Graft* being the most outrageous. (With her seventh letter, I felt the author would opt for a one-time bit of self-parody. Turned out she didn't. So what can I say? I was wrong.)

But that's the fun of the game. Being wrong can even be more fun than being right. Just consider the possibilities. *"N" Is for Nympho*—Kinsey goes undercover as a Playboy bunny. *"O" Is for Oscar*—Kinsey interrupts murder at the Academy Awards. *"P" Is for Poltergeist*—Kinsey is stranded in a Western ghost town.

See what I mean? None of those suggestions is ever likely to end up on a Grafton manuscript, but that's not the point of the game. It's just a silly and mindless way to spend a few happy minutes. And what's the harm?

Which brings me to *"S" Is for Stupid.* I have to admit that the title is not really part of the Grafton contest. It's more properly the epitaph for my headstone.

Somebody should have told me to stay in bed that fateful Thursday morning, pull the sheets up over my head, sleep straight through the next three days, and not wake again until Sunday.

At the very least.

But nobody was talking. Heck, even if I'd had forewarning, I doubt it would have done any good. 'Cause at the time I wasn't too big on listening. That's one of my problems—I've got a hard head. Granite and marble don't even come close to describing it. Just ask my wife, she'll tell you.

True, the first ten hours of that mid-October Thursday followed pretty much the same routine as do most of my days in Tipton, Connecticut, my home now for the past seven years which I share with my wife, Lee, my Irish setter, Bootsie, and my ferret, Wee (short for Weezer).

First thing that morning, I took Bootsie out for our regular daily run along the banks of the Yessula River, in the park which is located just across the street from my house. Then, somewhere around eleven o'clock, I finished my reading of the latest Dick Francis thriller, spent a couple of hours writing and polishing the review and then faxed it to the syndication service that distributes my reviews to newspapers around the country, enjoyed a late lunch with Lee, and even managed to catch a brief snooze on the living room sofa.

A pretty much Joe Average kind of day. Up to that point.

Then, about four-thirty in the afternoon, I foolishly yielded to an overwhelming and irresistible impulse. In other words, in a moment of duress, I blew it! Of course, at the time I truly believed I was making a sound decision. Yeah, hindsight's a real marvelous invention, all right. It can even zoom in on the fine print at the bottom of the eye chart. Fat lotta good it does!

Who knew? It was such a little thing, a minor infraction at worst, barely a blip on my life's radar screen. It's not like I stole the Crown Jewels, cheated on my income tax, rolled an old man in the park, or committed murder.

But it was strange how one rash yet seemingly inconsequential act, over the course of the next fifty or so hours, could so thoroughly disrupt the lives of several people, place my entire future in jeopardy, and startle me to the very core of my being.

Sure, I can say the words now, even repeat them. They're not exactly flattering to my ego, but they are nevertheless completely accurate—stupid, stupid, stupid.

Stupid.

Yes indeed, in retrospect there's absolutely no doubt I should have stayed in bed that Thursday morning.

Or to borrow a phrase forever associated with the great Mary Roberts Rinehart—

HAD I BUT KNOWN!

CHAPTER **TWO**

*"How the author
manages to get the reader
to put aside disbelief
and embrace
the impossible antics
of the animal characters
is perhaps this writer's
greatest marvel."*

—Stokes Moran,
on Lilian Jackson Braun's *The Cat Who Moved a Mountain*

"*S*tokes Moran must die!"

I don't usually lose my temper, but, on those rare occasions when I do, I sometimes tend to get overly dramatic. So I shouted those words with all the passion of a Marlon Brando impersonator, jumping up from the sofa and slamming my new book down against the seat cushions. I did everything but tear my shirt, pull my hair, and beat my chest.

"What is it now, Kyle?" Lee asked blandly from the other end of the sofa, a magazine in her lap and a box of chocolates and a can of cream soda at her fingertips.

My wife of eight months—who barely topped five feet in height and normally weighed no more than a hundred pounds soaking wet—had begun, in her seventh month of pregnancy, to add weight at such an alarmingly high rate that I was convinced she must be eating for sixteen rather than two. How she could possibly continue her present food consumption for another gluttonous eight weeks—until the December due date—posed a gastronomic puzzle worthy of Diane Mott Davidson, Katherine Hall Page, and Virginia Rich. On the one occasion when I had summoned my courage to broach the sensitive subject, Lee had downplayed my concern as "unnecessary husbandly worry," while she nevertheless continued to pack away the groceries.

But I was not presently preoccupied with Lee's predilection for calories. I could only see my own seemingly intolerable problem.

"Just look at this copy!" I yelled, hastily jerking the dust jacket off the discarded book. "After all my pleas and protestations, not a single reference to my real name, to Kyle Malachi!"

"So what's the problem?" Lee snagged the jacket I was wildly waving like a matador's cape in front of her face.

"That." I pointed to the offending jacket. "That's the problem."

"Don't get so worked up," she said, adjusting her reading glasses on the bridge of her nose. "Calm down for a minute and tell me just what it is that's so objectionable."

I took several measured breaths as Lee perused the wrapper text for *Alias Stokes Moran,* a collection of reviews, opinions, and essays I had written under my mystery-reviewing pseudonym. The hardcover coffee-table-sized book—at a hefty price tag of $35—was scheduled for national distribution the day after Thanksgiving, and the publisher had sent me an advance copy.

"I wanted my own name on the book," I objected simply. "In addition to my more famous pseudonym. I didn't think it would be such a big deal to just add a single line identifying Stokes Moran as Kyle Malachi."

"Kyle, I don't know what else you expected," Lee said.

"After all that unwanted publicity this past summer, I'd think you'd want to keep your two identities separate."

Back in May, and June, and continuing into August, I had unwillingly found myself in the international media spotlight. Kyle Malachi, sudden heir to the Holcomb millions. Or should I say billions? The murders had only fueled the feeding frenzy.* Luckily in the last few weeks interest had ebbed, and other scandals had happily diverted press attention away from me.

"That's definitely what the lawyers would prefer," I said. Then, adopting a falsetto voice, I paraphrased a fairly reasonable imitation of their legalistic lingo. *"Can't drag the hallowed family name into such an overtly crass enterprise as commercial publishing, especially not a mystery book."* I shook my head. "Oh my, no. Like the Holcomb name hadn't already been through more mud than the Hudson."

The doorbell rang, interrupting my discourse.

"Saved by the bell," Lee said, then laughed. "Uh-oh, here come the troops."

Irish setter and ferret bolted headlong out of the kitchen door, Bootsie barking out her cacophonous welcome, little Wee hard on her heels. I could never tell if the ferret actually understood that there was somebody at the front door, or if she was only responding to the dog's frenetic excitement. Acting on Lee's warning, I leaped ahead of the animal parade.

Ever since the ferret had joined our family group a few months back, even the simple act of opening an outside door had turned into a daily challenge. Crack the door an inch, and the tiny creature would be out and gone, possibly lost forever in the wilds of suburban Connecticut.

The little ferret had disrupted our household more than either Lee or I would ever have imagined possible. Our early and erroneous concern had centered on Wee's effect on Bootsie. After all, this house had been a canine kingdom for many

The Best Money Murder Can Buy (Scribner, 1996).

years. How would Bootsie react to a sudden usurper to her throne? But the dog had proved surprisingly receptive to the new houseguest, much more so than the two human inhabitants, whose lives the ferret seemed to take great delight in upsetting.

More curious than a cat, Wee demanded to know what was behind every shutter, inside every cabinet, and beneath every surface. She could be anywhere, at any time—on top of the television, inside the washing machine, under the La-Z-Boy recliner, or, particularly dangerous for Lee, on the stairs. Even such a menial chore as taking out the garbage had now assumed a terrifying new dimension. After having once found her unexpectedly asleep inside the trash bag, I no longer casually tossed the sacks out the back door. For Wee's sake, both Lee and I had learned to remain constantly vigilant.

I steadfastly refused to sentence her to a cage. Wee had enjoyed free run of her previous environment, and she deserved nothing less of her new home. Even if it sent me to an early grave. Which, judging from the nervous wreck Wee had turned me into, it very well might—and any day now at that.

The doorbell rang again before I could successfully snare the slippery ferret. "Just a minute," I yelled through the doorway to our unsuspecting visitor.

"No problem." The easily recognizable voice belonged to my next-door neighbor, Nolan James, who, through his frequent drop-overs, knew well the maneuver I was now engineering.

I finally scooped Wee up onto my shoulder, where she retained her perch while I laced my fingers through the dog's collar. This stooped posture had become so routine that I couldn't remember the last time I had been able to meet any visitor on an equal, eye-to-eye basis. It was giving me an inferiority complex, not to mention a perpetual backache.

With both animals under relatively reasonable restraint, I

turned the knob, releasing the lock. From the other side, Nolan pushed against the door and quickly sidled through the opening.

"Don't you ever get tired of all these shenanigans?" Nolan, as occasional baby-sitter to my animals, had personal knowledge of the physical exertions requisite in merely opening the door.

"Yes," I said. With the door safely closed and locked, I freed Bootsie from my grip and placed Wee gently back on the floor. Both animals immediately set upon Nolan, who suddenly looked like a helpless raccoon caught in the glaring headlights of an onrushing eighteen-wheeler.

"Down!" I commanded Bootsie, who had almost staggered Nolan under her eager assault, while the ferret nosed around Nolan's pant cuffs, preparatory to scaling the heights. Nolan had previously experienced the intimate indignity of Wee climbing all the way up the inside of his slacks. This time, Nolan shook her gently off his leg.

"Put the animals in the kitchen," Lee suggested with a trace of annoyance.

"It's okay," Nolan said, a grin spreading across his lips. "They're settling down."

And indeed they were. After the initial thrill had passed, Bootsie had plopped down on the floor beside the recliner and Wee had headed back to the kitchen.

"How do those two manage to get so worked up every time somebody comes to the door?" Nolan asked, leaning back into the La-Z-Boy.

"Visitors and food," Lee said sarcastically. "I think that's all they live for. Luckily, the ferret sleeps three hours out of every four. Which allows us mere mortals to rest up between skirmishes."

Nolan laughed. "Well, they're a pair, that's for sure. Oh," he added, unbuttoning his coat, "I ran into Freeman out front so I brought in your mail. Hope you don't mind."

He retrieved several envelopes and a single large package from inside his L. L. Bean hunting jacket. "I thought I'd keep 'em out of harm's way," he explained as he placed the items in my hands.

As a mystery reviewer, I get dozens of book deliveries a month. Those packages are normally too large to fit into the mailbox, which means Freeman, our regular carrier, must come to the door. Over the last few weeks, the wily mailman had become quite creative at avoiding unwanted animal contact. It would not have surprised me in the least if, contrary to all federal regulations, he had intentionally left our mail with Nolan. I couldn't blame him. After all, the UPS driver had started leaving all her deliveries on the outside stoop. Only her yet-to-wise-up substitute—on his infrequent forays into enemy territory—still braved the door.

The package Nolan handed over was not addressed to either Stokes Moran, book reviewer, or to Kyle Malachi, house occupant. Instead, it bore the Lee Holland Literary Agency name, which for the past half year had consisted of only one client—me.

"Uh-oh," I groaned, handing the package to my wife.

She nodded. "I'm afraid so," she said. "It looks like another return."

As Lee struggled with the strings and wrapping, I calculated that this was the fifth rejection of my manuscript in the last six weeks. For the past year, I had been working on my own mystery novel. Finally, two months ago, I had finished the first draft. After a little tinkering and polishing, I had handed the manuscript over to Lee, who also doubles as my agent, a function she performed long before we were ever married.

As agent to Stokes Moran, Lee had succeeded in syndicating my mystery reviews, with more than a hundred weekly and monthly subscribers all across the nation, ranging from

large metropolitan newspapers to monthly mystery periodi-
cals and fanzines. I supposed I now had the largest audience
of any single critic in America. Thanks to Lee.

She had not yet been quite so successful in selling my
novel, however. "It'd be a lot easier if you'd let me use your
name," she had frequently complained. "Either of your names,"
she had added pointedly.

From the first, I had insisted that the manuscript be sent out
without author identification. I wanted the book to be judged
on its own merits, and not have publishers swayed by either the
fame of Stokes Moran or the notoriety of Kyle Malachi—the
"Holcomb Heir." Thus far, the gambit had backfired.

It was a no-win situation. Over the last year, I had grown
increasingly frustrated with my Stokes Moran alter ego,
especially when the publisher of *Alias Stokes Moran* had
consistently refused to acknowledge my true identity. Then,
with all the media furor following the Holcomb affair, I could
no longer use the name Kyle Malachi even to order a pizza.
It had become almost as well known a sobriquet as O. J.
Simpson.

With five straight rejections, though, I was beginning
to wonder if my no-name mystery novel held any appeal
whatsoever.

"Don't worry, Kyle," Lee said as she slid the manuscript
out of the cardboard container. "It's just a matter of finding
the right publisher. And, believe me, we will."

As former literary agent for dozens of published writers—
a couple of whom consistently made the best-seller lists—
Lee recognized quality when she saw it, and she thought my
book was good. But as she had said immediately after she had
first read it: "The question's not so much is it good as is it
commercial."

The telephone rang. Lee picked it up.

"Yes."

A rare condition for him, Nolan had lapsed into companionable silence, his short, wiry frame draped haphazardly against the recliner. Nolan, an ex-cop, had been my nextdoor neighbor on this quiet cul-de-sac in Tipton for almost three years.

Best not to think too much about those events, though. At least not at the moment. So I sorted through the rest of the mail while half listening to my wife's side of the telephone conversation.

"This is she." Pause. "Yes, I see."

I could tell it was a business call. Prior to her pregnancy, Lee had confined all her professional activities to her Manhattan apartment, which she still owned and until recently had continued to visit two or three times a week in order to handle her clients. But following the advice of her obstetrician, she had cut back on the commute—first to once a week, and then, some two months ago, to just once a month. Because of that travel restriction, she had been obliged to conduct business, for a while at least, out of our Tipton home.

"Thanks for calling," she concluded. "Yes, I'll let him know immediately."

Lee closed the portable phone and placed it on the cushion next to her. She opened her mouth to speak, then stopped. I looked at her with growing curiosity and not a little bit of suspicion.

"What is it?" I asked.

Lee pushed herself up off the sofa and walked over behind Nolan, aligning the chair and the coffee table between us.

"It's good news," she said somewhat meekly.

"Oh?" I left the sofa as well, joining my wife behind the recliner. Nolan was forced to crane his neck just to keep us in his line of vision.

"It is," Lee reiterated, and nodded her head for emphasis.

"Then why don't you tell me about it?" I said.

She sighed, then blurted, "Galaxy Press has bought your book."

My heart lurched, but I knew there was more to the story, otherwise Lee wouldn't be acting so cagey.

"That's wonderful," I said, curbing my initial enthusiasm. "Now why don't you tell me the rest of it."

"Rest of it?" Lee tried to appear nonchalant. "I don't know what you mean."

I draped my arm around her shoulder. "Sure you do. There's something you're not telling me—something you're intentionally not telling me—and we both know it."

Lee transferred her gaze from me to Nolan. "Nolan, would you like a cup of coffee? I'll be glad to get it for you."

"Sure—"

"Shut up, Nolan," I said, perhaps just a tad too sharply. "We're generating enough of a caffeine buzz right here." With my left hand, I cupped my wife's chin and turned her face toward mine. "Now, Lee, tell me what it is that you so obviously don't want to tell me."

I saw a tear form in the corner of her left eye. "It's good news, really it is."

"You already said that."

"Kyle—" She stopped.

"Yes."

"I identified the author as Stokes Moran."

"What!" I stepped away from my wife. "How could you? I specifically forbade you to do that."

"I know," she said, "but the book is good. I knew any publisher would love to get it."

"Only if it's by Stokes Moran," I said.

"It doesn't matter. Hundreds of good books are rejected every year. I couldn't stand by and watch while your book went down the tubes. Stokes Moran makes it commercial. Why can't you see that?"

I stormed over to the sofa and picked the phone up from

where Lee had left it. I dialed directory information in Manhattan.

"Kyle, what are you doing?" Lee demanded. "You're not calling Galaxy Press, are you? Please don't do anything rash."

"No, I'm not calling Galaxy," I said. "I'm—" The operator's voice sounded in my ear. "Give me the number for *The New York Times*," I requested.

Lee walked over to where I stood. "Kyle?" she asked, a puzzled expression visible on her face.

I waved her silent, repeating in my head the number I had just been given. I punched it into the keypad.

"*Times?*" I asked. "Connect me with Obituaries."

Lee frowned. "Kyle, please tell me what you're doing!" Her voice sounded frantic.

"I'm killing off Stokes Moran. Once and for all."

CHAPTER **THREE**

*"Something as commonplace
as the ringing
of a bell
can
trigger
unforeseen changes
in the lives of all concerned."*

—Stokes Moran,
on Nancy Pickard's *Confession*

$\mathcal{T}$he death notice appeared the following morning, though not in the Obituary section as I had expected. Instead, the newspaper placed the announcement in its "Chronicle" column hidden deep inside the Metro section. It was a simple two-sentence statement under the headline MORAN IS DEAD: *"The Times* has been informed that nationally syndicated mystery critic Stokes Moran has died. No further details were immediately available."

"You're going to regret it," Lee said, carefully folding the newspaper and placing it next to her empty breakfast plate on the kitchen table.

"Maybe." Sitting across from my wife, I gripped both hands around my Murder Ink commemorative mug and gulped the steaming black coffee, scalding my mouth in the process. I didn't care about the damage to my tongue or tonsils, I needed the caffeine. Desperately.

Seeing Stokes Moran's death announced in cold print had unnerved me, much more than I had anticipated. I was momentarily experiencing a sick feeling in the pit of my stomach that I couldn't quite describe. It wasn't exactly dread, or shock, or panic. But it was close. I wondered if this was how Sir Arthur Conan Doyle had felt when he killed off Sherlock Holmes at Reichenbach Falls. Had I, as Lee maintained, acted too rashly?

"He can always rise from the dead," I said, recalling the Great Detective's miraculous return to Baker Street following the loud public outcry over the author's 1891 short story, "The Final Problem."

"What?"

"Stokes Moran. I can resurrect him."

"He's not a fictional character," Lee said, as if reading my thoughts, "that you can just bring back to life as if nothing happened. Besides, you forget I confirmed the story."

I had not forgotten. The afternoon before, as soon as I had disconnected the call to the newspaper, Lee had descended on me in lionesslike fury, which Nolan observed in helpless silence.

"Kyle, are you crazy?" she'd shouted. "You've spent the better part of a decade establishing the Stokes Moran name, not to mention all the time and effort I've devoted to building the syndication network. Now you've thrown it all away. I can't believe it!"

"I was fed up," I'd said, trying to match my wife's hostility. But, now the deed was done, I found that my anger was quickly dissipating.

"And what about the book?"

"Which one?"

"Either one!" she'd yelled. "You've put both of them in

jeopardy." Lee sat down on the sofa and crossed both arms over her chest. "Or don't you care about being published anymore?"

I looked to Nolan for support, but he just despairingly shook his head. Before I could mount a defense, the phone rang.

"Hello?" Lee's greeting was overtly curt. "Yes, this is she."

With my wife's anger momentarily focused elsewhere, I reflected on my impulsive act. Maybe Lee was right, that I had overreacted, that I had not fully thought through the consequences, but, dammit, I was sick and tired of Stokes Moran getting all the credit. After all, he was my creation. I had every right to kill him off if that's what I wanted.

"Kyle!" Lee waved frantically for my attention, cupping her hand over the telephone's mouthpiece. "This is *The New York Times*. They want me to confirm Stokes Moran's death."

Startled, I asked, "Why did they call you?"

"They tracked me down," she answered. "They know I'm his agent."

"How?"

Lee looked at me as if I were a retarded child. "It's a matter of public record."

"I know, but how did they get to you this fast? Oh, never mind."

"What do you want me to say?"

"Tell them Stokes Moran is dead," I said.

Lee frowned. "Are you sure you want to do this? It isn't too late to change your mind. I could deny the report. Say it was a hoax or something."

"No." I adamantly shook my head. "I've made my decision."

Still frowning, Lee lifted her hand from the mouthpiece. "Yes," she said, but I could hear the reluctance in her voice, "that's the information I have. Stokes Moran is dead. I'm sorry, that's all I can tell you at this time. No, I don't have any of the details."

The rest of the evening had lapsed into an uneasy truce between Lee and me, the two of us barely communicating anything more significant than the choice of dinner entree. Nolan had taken his leave from the war zone sometime around seven-thirty. I couldn't blame him. After all, being caught in the middle of a domestic dispute can lead to fatal consequences.

Wee's cold nose, touching my bare ankle, jerked me suddenly back to the breakfast table and the present predicament. Lee looked at me expectantly.

"What?" I asked.

"I said, what are you going to do now?"

I stood up, carrying my mug with me. "For starters, I'm going to have another cup of coffee."

"Kyle, you're absolutely impossible," Lee said, shaking her head. "Will you get me a decaffeinated one, too?" She lifted her cup in my direction.

I poured us two steaming cups. Following at my heels, Wee detoured to her food bowl and started crunching on her country mix cat food. Bootsie lay curled up on the kitchen rug, glaring jealously at the ferret.

"Sorry, old girl," I addressed my dog as I headed back to the table, "it's not my fault you've already scarfed down your breakfast."

"Thanks," Lee said as I handed her the refill. "Seriously, Kyle, what are you going to do now?"

"I don't know," I answered simply as I reclaimed my seat.

Stokes Moran had become almost a living presence in my life during the past decade. It was strangely schizophrenic the way I viewed him as an identifiable entity, separate and apart from the person I was. But there was no getting around it. He was me! And maybe I was him, more even than I cared to admit. Otherwise, it didn't make any sense why I was feeling this heavy constriction in my chest, this darkness that continued to cloud my vision. Could it possibly be grief? Stokes Moran was nothing more than a pseudonym, my pseudonym. He was not and never had been a real person. I knew that, had told myself that repeatedly over the years, and yet here I was, consciously mourning his death—the death of a name. It was crazy!

"I made a mistake." I whispered the words, softly breaking the silence.

Lee slammed her cup down on the tabletop. Startled by the unexpected noise, Wee scurried toward the living room doorway, sliding around the final turn and disappearing into the next room.

"Good, now maybe we can undo the damage."

I pondered the depths of my coffee. "What do you suggest?"

"First," Lee said, pushing back her chair and rising to her feet, "I'll call the *Times* and say that, just like them, I too was misled by bad information."

"Do you think they'll believe that?"

"When I put you on the line as Stokes Moran, they will."

"Won't it hurt your credibility that you confirmed an erroneous story?"

"Possibly, but I'm not going to worry about that right now. The most important thing is to correct that story before it goes any further."

But before Lee could make the call, the telephone rang. Lee answered.

I was grateful Lee had sprung into immediate action and avoided any I-told-you-so's. Not that she didn't have a right. I had definitely compromised her reputation with one of the most influential publications in America, and I could only hope that no lasting harm would result from my irresponsible act. I vowed that my love-hate relationship with my alter identity would cease as of this moment. Like it or not, Stokes Moran and I were joined at the hip, as intertwined and interdependent as Siamese twins. Forever.

Just like Doyle and Holmes, and look what happened there. Of course, Sir Arthur wasn't the only mystery writer ever to kill off his series detective, just the first and certainly the most notable. But there have been others.

I wondered if Nicholas Freeling had experienced a similar metamorphosis back in 1972 when he assassinated his internationally respected creation Commissaris Piet Van der Valk, in *Auprès de ma Blonde*. Ever after, the author had seemed to me somewhat less interesting, less energized. Had Freeling somehow lost an essential part of himself when he wrote the end of his famous character?

Maybe that's why, after finishing off Hercule Poirot in *Curtain*, Agatha Christie hid the book in a bank vault for more than thirty years. By ignoring the existence of Poirot's scripted death—by deliberately postponing it until nearer the time of her own demise—had Christie unconsciously been extending her own survival? At least as a writer?

Perhaps it's best that writers not tempt mortality by killing off their fictional characters, their alter identities. Nero Wolfe has definitely outlived Rex Stout and today enjoys new adventures under the authorship of Robert Goldsborough. Cousins Frederic Dannay and Manfred Lee surely wouldn't have even contemplated the death of Ellery Queen, since they also wrote under that pen name. Had they murdered Ellery Queen, it would have been tantamount to suicide. Maybe that's what was bothering me most about my action. Had I, in killing off Stokes Moran, committed an unwitting form of suicide? Could I conceivably possess a secret death wish?

I failed to catch Lee's final words, but I saw her face. The color had faded from her cheeks.

"What is it?" I stood up and walked over to where she was standing. "What's wrong?"

"That was the New York City police," she said, snapping

the transmitter closed and disconnecting the call. "They want me to come down and identify the body."

"The body," I repeated in astonishment. "Whose body?"

My wife's eyes met mine with a perplexed stare. "Stokes Moran's."

CHAPTER **FOUR**

*"The female lead
is a perfect foil,
performing
most of the legwork
and also inheriting the lion's share
of the trouble."*

—Stokes Moran,
on D. J. Donaldson's *New Orleans Requiem*

"*H*ow did I manage to get into such a mess?" I asked forlornly.

The question was of course rhetorical, but Lee couldn't resist another gibe.

"You're stupid, that's how."

Throughout the hour-long drive down from Tipton, my wife and I had discussed and debated the improbable—the outrageously impossible—situation we now faced. Twenty-four hours ago, my biggest problem had been my self-admitted loathing and jealousy of Stokes Moran. Since then, I had killed off the pseudonymous nemesis, had placed the announcement of his death in *The New York Times,* and had unintentionally involved my wife in a public fraud. But all of that was small potatoes compared with the fact that we were now on our way to identify the body of a man who supposedly didn't exist.

The police would not be thrilled.

Lee had agreed to meet Detective Lockwood—the New York City policeman who had phoned—at the City Morgue at noon, which had given us little more than ninety minutes to get downtown. We had quickly dressed, separated the animals—disaster would have resulted had we left them together, so Bootsie got the run of the kitchen while Wee was exiled to the upstairs bedroom—and jumped in the Land Rover with Lee behind the wheel. Lee had opted for the Boston Post Road instead of the expressways, and we had made fairly good time until we hit the outskirts of New York City. Now, stalled in traffic on the Bronx side of the Willis Avenue Bridge, we had less than fifteen minutes to reach our eventual destination. There was no way we'd make our appointment on time.

"Have you decided what you're going to tell the cops?" I asked after several moments of silence.

"Me? You're the one responsible for all this."

"Yes, but they asked for you."

"Only because they don't know about Kyle Malachi, alias Stokes Moran." I could hear the sarcastic overtones in my wife's voice, especially in the last three words. But I couldn't fault her anger. I certainly deserved it.

"We can't tell them the truth," I said. "They'd never believe it."

Lee laughed. "You've got that right."

"So what do we do?"

"Have you given any thought to the possibility that this man's name really could be Stokes Moran?"

"Of course it's possible," I said, then shook my head. "But I don't think it's very likely. For one thing, in all the time I've used the name, I've never run across another Stokes Moran. For another, it's just too much of a coincidence. Stokes

Moran's death was announced only in this morning's newspaper. Then presto—a dead body turns up bearing his name a scant few hours later. No, it's just too preposterous to be believable."

"I agree with that." Lee, looking like a pregnant triangle wedged between the steering wheel and the seat, shifted into gear and the car surged forward under the signal light, onto the bridge over the Harlem River, and into upper Manhattan.

"But the alternative seems even more bizarre. How could a dead body be identified as Stokes Moran?" I paused. "Did the police say what it was that led them to that assumption?"

"No."

"Did they say how they knew to call you?"

"Yes." Lee nodded. "Detective Lockwood explained that either he or one of his men—I can't remember exactly which—had seen the report in this morning's newspaper. So he called *The New York Times*, and one of the editors gave him my name and telephone number."

"Does he know what your relationship to Stokes Moran is?" I asked.

Lee frowned. "I'm not even sure I know the answer to that one." Then she laughed. "Do you?"

I ignored my wife's gentle rebuke. I was still trying to figure out what to do. In a matter of minutes, Lee and I would be facing the police and their questions. I too had questions. Lots of questions. I just didn't have any of the answers.

The morgue—or, as it more properly boasts in large lettering on the front of the bluish-gray concrete structure: "Office of the Medical Examiner, City of New York"—sits on the southwest corner of First Avenue and Thirtieth Street, across from—actually dwarfed by—the sprawling Bellevue Hospital complex. Separated from the East River by the FDR Drive, the building is the final stop for New York City dead this side of the hereafter.

Since First Avenue is a one-way street heading north, we'd had to come down Second Avenue and cut back across on Twenty-ninth. Lee pulled the Land Rover next to the right curb and parked behind an NYPD blue-and-white cruiser. A coroner's wagon headed the line.

"You'll get towed," I warned as I joined Lee on the broad sidewalk.

"We're on police business," Lee answered, dropping her car keys into her handbag.

"Sure," I said with a straight face. "Try telling that to the judge."

We climbed a couple of steps and entered the double-plated glass doors, finding ourselves in a cadaver-friendly lobby that smelled suspiciously antiseptic. The carpeted floor did little to dispel the effect.

"I hate this odor," I whispered. "It's just like a hospital."

"Not quite," Lee said. "These patients never complain about the service."

Two men in buttoned-down collars and pin-striped suits—one navy, the other charcoal gray—headed directly toward us. One towered over the other.

"Miss Holland?" asked the charcoal gray. Astonishingly tall—at least six-five, maybe even six-six—muscular—he obviously outweighed me by an easy seventy-five pounds, not an ounce of which was fat—and sporting a freshly scalped haircut, the man loomed over the five-foot Lee like a line-backer over a football. Make that a pregnant football.

"Mrs. Malachi," Lee corrected, then nodded in my direction. "And this is my husband, Kyle. Detective Lockwood?"

"Right," said charcoal gray. "And this is my partner, Detective John Pride." Navy acknowledged the introduction with a phantom smile that touched his eyes but not his lips. He was a good six inches shorter than his partner, with a sparse frame that was topped with a curly mane of black hair.

"Thank you for coming on such short notice," Lockwood said. Walking inconceivably on the balls of his feet, he gave every appearance of a giant sequoia ready to topple. Lee and I obediently followed in his footsteps, but just beyond potential "timber!" range. "I know it's not a pleasant prospect," he added, "identifying a body. It's a chore most people never experience in their entire lifetimes."

Lockwood led us past the receptionist's desk and turned right down a long polished tile corridor, passing door after unidentified door. No one spoke again until Lockwood finally stopped in front of one of these doors on the left side of the hallway.

"You didn't say much on the phone," Lee said as Lockwood ushered us into a sparsely furnished room with only a table and some chairs giving evidence that activity of any kind took place here. Along the wall to our left, a waist-high window extended from corner to corner. One could only imagine what lay behind the drawn white curtain that closed off the view. "How can you be so sure it's Mr. Moran?"

"We found some identification among the victim's personal effects," Detective Lockwood said as my wife and I settled uneasily into two of the hard-backed chairs. Both detectives remained standing. "You say victim," Lee said. "What do you mean by victim?"

"Let's wait until after you see the body."

Both Lee and I looked instinctively toward the interior window, as if waiting for the parting of the Red Sea. Instead, Lockwood reached inside his coat pocket and pulled out a large folded envelope and tossed it on the table in front of us.

"I don't understand—" Lee began.

Lockwood smiled. "Everybody makes the same assumption. But we use photo identification now. You don't actually have to view the body."

Lee and I sighed in unison—too soon. "Unless the photos don't do the job," Lockwood added.

I detected only the slightest tremble in my wife's hands as she lifted the envelope and shook out its contents. The three pictures emerged face up, revealing from various angles the head and upper torso of a man I knew I had never before seen.

"Well?" Lockwood asked. "Is that Stokes Moran?"

Lee looked at me. "I—" she started.

"Take your time, Mrs. Malachi," said Lockwood. "I know this isn't easy."

"It's not that," Lee said, breathing deeply. "It's just—" Again, my wife left her words hanging.

"Just what?"

Lee summoned her courage and plunged into the explanation. "Just that I don't know if that's Stokes Moran or not."

Lockwood frowned. "You mean you can't make a positive ID from the photos?"

"No, it's not that," Lee said, shaking her head. "Detective Lockwood, I don't have the least idea who that man is. The only Stokes Moran I know is not dead. He's very much alive, at least until I can kill him"—Lee gave me a murderous look—"and he's sitting right here next to me. Let me introduce him. It's my husband, Kyle Malachi. Alias Stokes Moran." She ended her pronouncement with a sardonic little cough, added intentionally, I was certain, for my benefit alone.

Both policemen looked at me in obvious confusion. Right then I wished I were dead.

"Maybe we should go down to the precinct house and talk this over?" suggested Detective Lockwood as the four of us walked back toward the front entrance.

Lee stopped in mid-stride. "Look, my husband and I don't

know anything about this man's death, I can promise you that."

Lockwood looked at Lee sternly. "Maybe you do, and maybe you don't," he said. "But right now, you're the only leads we have."

"Leads?" I asked incredulously. "Are you accusing us of a crime?"

"Look," Lee said, placing her right hand on Lockwood's upper arm, "I can assure you that we have no information. But we'll be happy to tell you everything we can. Just, could we do it somewhere else, like in a coffee shop?"

Lockwood gave Lee a smile. "I think that could be arranged."

"Carmine's is right around the corner." Pride spoke for the first time.

As the four of us jaywalked across the street, I was pleased to see that the Land Rover still sat behind the police car. Maybe the fact that it had not yet been towed would serve as an omen for Lee and me, that good fortune would be with us. I certainly hoped so.

We were soon all sitting at a back table amid a very large and very noisy lunchtime crowd. By sheer volume, Carmine's had to be counted a success. There were at least a couple of hundred people jammed into the two dining rooms, not to count the several dozen standing in the bar. I glanced at the menu. At these prices, I thought, Carmine's owners ought to be able to bankroll Chase Manhattan.

A waitress in a pressed pink uniform and starched white collar approached the table, pen poised expectantly over her order pad.

"Okay, folks, what'll it be?"

"Four coffees—three regular, one decaffeinated," said Lockwood.

"Come on, give me a break, Daddy Warbucks. I got people waitin' to eat here."

Lockwood flipped open his shield. The waitress took one

look at the shiny badge, muttered, "Aw crap, just my luck," and stormed away.

"Detective," Lee said, "I do believe you've made a conquest."

"She's just afraid she won't get much of a tip."

"Is she right?"

"She is now," Lockwood said with a grin.

"Everything's on me," I said. "Including the tip."

"In that case," said Pride, "I'll have the prime rib."

We all laughed. Lockwood reminded his partner, "Just coffee," and by the time the coffee finally arrived, Lee had pretty much filled the two policemen in on the history of our Stokes Moran.

"So either there's no connection at all," Lee concluded, "or—"

"I don't believe in coincidence," said Lockwood.

"Neither do I," I said.

"Or," Lee persisted, "somebody's involved who also knows that Kyle is Stokes Moran."

"Besides the two of you, who might that be?" asked Lockwood.

Lee shrugged. "There could be dozens, hundreds of people."

"I thought you said the name was a secret."

"Not a secret," I explained. "A pseudonym. But not a closely guarded one like K. C. Constantine or Seymour Severe."*

"I'm sorry," Lockwood said. "You've lost me."

"Never mind," I said. "My editor knows, my publicist, my syndicators, other people in the publishing business, my friends. They all know I'm Stokes Moran."

"Plus you've occasionally traveled under that name as well," Lee reminded me.

"In other words," Lockwood said, "there are potentially a lot of people who have access to that knowledge?"

*Otherwise Known As Murder (Scribner, 1994).

40

I nodded. "And who knows who those people might have told. It could be hundreds."

Lockwood ran his hands over his stubbled head. "I'm beginning to see the problem." He paused. "But no one knew you were planning to kill off Stokes Moran?"

"That's right." I leaned across the table. "I didn't even know myself. Not until yesterday afternoon. It was a spur-of-the-moment kind of thing."

"It was stupid," said Lee, nodding in agreement, "but not criminal."

Lockwood shook his head vigorously. "None of this makes any sense. A man's body—with papers identifying him as Stokes Moran—was found at eight o'clock this morning, just hours after the newspaper announcing Stokes Moran's death hit the streets. Now how is something like that possible?"

"Maybe the guy had been masquerading as me for quite some time," I suggested.

Lockwood looked me squarely in the eye. "Why?"

"I don't know," I answered. "Perhaps it's some sort of con."

"Oh really. Has anybody attempted to shake you down recently?"

"No." I stopped, then had a sudden inspiration. "But maybe the scheme was still in the early planning stages."

"What do you mean?" asked Lockwood.

"My husband is about to inherit a very large sum of money," said Lee, correctly divining my line of thought.

"How much money?" Pride asked.

"Somewhere in the vicinity of a billion dollars," answered Lee.

"Whew!" both detectives exclaimed in chorus.

"Now that's definitely a motive for murder," said Lockwood.

"Murder?" Lee and I chimed together.

"Don't you think it's time you told us what this is all about?" Lee directed her question at Lockwood, who appeared somewhat uncomfortable with the direct appeal.

"Yes," he said finally. "It's either that or read you your rights. You two are still the only suspects I have," Lockwood said, then added with an impish grin, "for the moment, that is."

I decided to put an awful lot of faith in that lopsided grin.

CHAPTER **FIVE**

*"The author
makes the point
that monumental events
turn on minor whims,
that people's lives are predestined
by simple choices
made in the course of a single day."*

—Stokes Moran,
on Dick Francis's *Decider*

"*T*he body was discovered today around eight A.M.," Lockwood explained. "A total fluke, really."

"What do you mean?" I asked.

The detective laughed. "A tenant in the Mansard Building—it's one of those old Art Deco monstrosities just off Eleventh and Broadway—arrived early for work this morning. After she had started the coffee brewing, she decided to water her hibiscus plant. In the process, she overdid it. Too lazy, I suppose, to walk halfway down the hall to the bathroom, she opened the window and turned the plant over to drain off the excess water. When she did that, the plant slid out of the pot and fell six stories to the ground below. Dismayed, the woman looked over the window ledge, and that's when she spotted the body."

"I don't suppose it had been there long?" said my wife.

"Not long at all," Lockwood answered. "And that's the irony. Under normal circumstances, the body might have remained undiscovered for days. In fact, a few years ago another body went undiscovered for a couple of weeks at that same location."

"What do you mean?" I felt as if I were constantly repeating myself. "This is Manhattan. How could a body go that long without discovery?"

Lockwood smiled. "Easy, if you know this building. You see, two of the building's external walls abut directly up against two of the external walls from the adjacent building, thereby forming an open air shaft approximately ten feet square. The windows looking out on the air shaft on the bottom five floors of both buildings are blacked out and nailed shut—for what purpose, I have no idea, maybe someone's notion of security—but from the sixth floor on up, the windows are clear and can still be opened. But from that height, somebody'd have to stick his head all the way out of the window in order to see the ground."

"And that's just what happened," I said.

Lockwood nodded. "And bad timing for the killer. This way, the evidence is still fresh."

"Then you're sure the man was murdered?" asked Lee. "And that it couldn't have been just some kind of terrible accident?"

"Oh, he was murdered, all right. He had a deep puncture wound in his chest. That's what stopped his heart, or so says the unofficial coroner's finding."

"But couldn't he have sustained that injury if, say, he fell from one of the upper floors?" Lee asked.

Lockwood shook his head. "There was no blood on the ground. Neither was there anything found at the scene that could explain such a wound. But we'll have a more complete picture after the autopsy is completed."

Lee frowned. "I thought, especially since you had us meet you at the morgue, that the autopsy had already been concluded."

"We're fast, but we're not that fast." Lockwood grinned. "When I called you at ten-thirty, the coroner's wagon had just collected the body from the scene. I then phoned the assistant ME and asked her not to start the autopsy until after you'd had a chance to identify the body."

"Sparing our sensibilities, no doubt," Lee said.

I promise you Lockwood actually blushed. I hadn't observed that phenomenon in an adult male in years. "The autopsy probably wouldn't have been scheduled until later this afternoon or tomorrow morning at the earliest, not with our current backlog of cases. I just thought it best not to take the chance."

"Thank you," Lee said. "It's nice to know chivalry isn't dead." My wife gave me a withering look.

The thoroughly embarrassed detective cleared his throat, then shifted his eyes to the waitress removing dirty dishes from the adjoining table. "Hey, miss," he called, pointing at the coffee cups. "You think we could have some refills?" Then, ignoring the waitress's stony stare and focusing his attention once again on Lee, Lockwood continued, "But, even without the autopsy, we do know the man was definitely dead before he fell."

"He fell too?" Not even Diane Sawyer could have been as guileless as my wife.

"There's no access into the air shaft. It's open to the sky, but that's all. The first unit on the scene had to break out one of the ground-floor windows just to get to the body."

"Then—" I began, but Lockwood interrupted my speculation.

"Someone threw it there," he said with an affirmative nod, "just like an old bag of trash."

• • •

Four more coffees finally arrived, courtesy of the unfriendly waitress, and I noticed that Carmine's lunchtime crowd was beginning to thin out. I glanced at my watch and realized we'd been sitting around this table for more than an hour. By this time, I feared that the Land Rover was probably halfway to the car impound lot.

"Why don't we walk as we talk," I suggested, hurriedly draining my fresh cup.

"Good idea," said Lee.

"Fine with us," agreed Lockwood, speaking for his partner as well. "The atmosphere's a little chilly in here anyway." He glared at the retreating waitress. "Of course, there's nothing quite like service with a smile."

Leaving a two-dollar tip anyway, I picked up the check and carried it with me to the front cash register. Three minutes later, and temporarily blinded by the startling contrast from Carmine's dim interior to the bright October sunshine, I joined Lee and the two detectives on the sidewalk.

"What now?" I asked, shielding my eyes against the concrete glare.

Lockwood shrugged. "You tell us."

Lee answered. "You still haven't mentioned what it was that specifically identified the man as Stokes Moran." The four of us slowly ambled toward First Avenue.

"It was this," Lockwood said, reaching inside his coat pocket, producing a black fold-over wallet, and extending it toward Lee. Abruptly, the four of us came to a dead stop in the middle of the busy sidewalk, but the other pedestrians merely bypassed us without the least sign of curiosity or irritation.

"Is it all right for me to touch it?" Lee asked suspiciously.

Lockwood laughed. "Go ahead, it won't bite you. We already checked it anyway." Lee carefully lifted the wallet from the detective's hand as Lockwood continued the explanation. "It was wiped clean. There were no fingerprints at all, not even the dead man's."

"That proves it!" I said. "Somebody must have planted it on him."

"Either that," Lockwood said, "or, after taking the victim's money, the killer was smart enough to remove his prints."

"Then you know he was robbed?" I asked.

Lockwood shook his head. "No, I don't. But there was no money found in his wallet. Adult men usually don't walk around New York without at least a little cash."

"But if the killer took the man's money," Lee said, "then why did he leave Stokes Moran's credit card?"

"What!" I grabbed the Visa card out of my wife's hand. Sure enough, the name Stokes Moran was clearly imprinted on the front.

"Was that card issued to you, Mr. Malachi?" Lockwood asked. The imaginary noose tightened around my Adam's apple.

"No! Of course not!"

"Do you have any credit cards in the name of Stokes Moran?"

"I—" I couldn't form the words. Lee intervened on my behalf.

"Yes," she said, "my husband has occasionally traveled as Stokes Moran. When he does, he uses the American Express card."

"Then the AmEx card is in the name Stokes Moran?" Lockwood asked.

"Yes," I said irritably. "But I don't see what that proves."

Lockwood didn't respond. He just gave me an assessing stare.

"What else is in that wallet?" I asked with increasing nervousness.

"Well," Lee answered, pulling out the contents, handing

each item to me in turn. "There's a social security card, a video rental card, a library card, a supplemental health insurance card—"

All bore the Stokes Moran name. "But there's no driver's license," I shouted when Lee had ended the inventory. "Nothing with a photo. Anybody could have produced these."

"In only a few hours?" Lockwood sounded skeptical. "In the middle of the night?"

I didn't know how to answer, so I kept my mouth shut. The warning "You have the right to remain silent" echoed ominously in my head. I expected Lockwood to speak those words for real at any moment.

"Then you don't recognize any of these items?" Lockwood asked, lifting the cards from my hands. "Not a single one belongs to you?"

I shook my head vehemently. "No! Absolutely not. I've never seen any of them before."

Lockwood folded the wallet and slipped it back inside his jacket. "We'll see," he said enigmatically.

"Look, I'll show you." I reached into my front pants pocket and withdrew my money clip. "See. Here's my social security card," I said, thrusting the plastic toward Lockwood's face.

He took both the card and the clip, squinting as he said, "This says Kyle Malachi."

"Of course it says Kyle Malachi. What should it say? George Pataki?" Fear and frustration were making me reckless.

"Do you have with you the American Express card your wife referred to that identifies you as Stokes Moran?" Lockwood inquired.

"No, of course not," I answered. "It's in my bureau drawer at home. I only carry it at certain times, when I expect to use it."

"And you haven't used it anytime lately?"

"No."

"Then you wouldn't normally carry Stokes Moran's social security card either."

"Stokes Moran doesn't have a social security card," I nearly screamed.

"What my husband means," Lee said, "is that he doesn't have a separate social security card under that name. His income and his taxes are all reported in his real name, Kyle Malachi."

I expelled a pent-up breath. "Thank you, Lee. That's exactly what I meant."

"Then these items weren't stolen from you?" Lockwood asked, gazing directly into my eyes.

"I've already told you, no. If there's not another Stokes Moran somewhere, then somebody had them purposely counterfeited."

"Why?"

"How should I know? All I do know is that these are not my cards. How many times do I have to say it?" I rubbed the bridge of my nose.

"Until I believe you," Lockwood said flatly.

I clenched my right hand, stifling the urge to smash my fist into his smug face. Given Lockwood's gargantuan size, I recognized not only the futility of such a gesture but also its inherent danger. I'd surely end up behind bars, and with a bruised body to boot.

The four of us walked the next block and a half in an uneasy silence. As we rounded the corner of Thirtieth and First, I spotted the Land Rover on the far side of the street still parked snugly behind the police cruiser; it had not been towed away after all. At least something had gone right with my day.

While waiting for the signal to change, Lockwood asked, "Where will you two be going now?"

"Back home, I guess," my wife answered.

"To Connecticut?"

Lee and I nodded in unison.

"Don't," Lockwood said.

"Why?" I asked.

"Let's just say it'd be better if you stayed in town for the time being."

I started to protest, but my wife intervened. "I have an apartment on the Upper West Side. Kyle and I can stay there, at least temporarily." Lee nodded and smiled at me encouragingly.

"Oh, all right," I agreed. "I guess I can get Nolan to take care of the animals. At least for a little while," I added with emphasis.

Lee opened her handbag, removed one of her business cards, and handed it to the detective. "That's the address and phone number. You can reach us there. And if by chance we're away from the apartment, you can leave a message with my answering service."

"Good." Lockwood grinned, slipping the card into his inside coat pocket. He then offered Lee one of his cards. "I really appreciate your cooperation," he said after the mutual exchange of cards had been completed, "both of you." Who did he think he was kidding? I had eyes; I could see that his gratitude extended only to Lee.

The light changed, and the four of us crossed the street in single file. As we reached the Land Rover, Lee fished the car keys out of her bag.

"You really have to be careful in this city," Lockwood warned. "Lockup can be quite expensive."

Was he talking about the car? Or me?

We exchanged good-byes, and the two detectives headed toward the morgue entrance. Just before I climbed into the passenger seat, I called out to Lockwood, "Your partner doesn't say very much, does he?"

Halfway up the sidewalk, Lockwood turned on his toes, walking backward for a few steps, but still keeping pace with Pride. "No, I guess he doesn't," the detective laughed, "but he sure does see a lot."

Yes, I thought, I just bet he does.

CHAPTER **SIX**

"Through the character
of her engaging detective,
the author
affords us the opportunity
to glimpse how alike we really are,
no matter how loudly
we may protest."

—Stokes Moran,
on Barbara D'Amato's *Hard Bargain*

"*H*e thinks I did it," I said, once Lee had successfully merged the Land Rover into the mid-afternoon traffic, heading north on First.

"Who?"

"Who do you think?" I asked in amazement. "Lockwood, of course."

"Nonsense," Lee said, braking for a FedEx van that suddenly veered into the inside lane.

"It's not nonsense at all," I said. "If you hadn't been so captivated by the man's unctuous charm, you'd have realized I'm his prime suspect."

"Charm?" Lee gave me a brief glance. "Kyle, you've got to be kidding."

"I am not kidding. I saw how he ogled you."

Lee laughed. "I'm seven months pregnant, for crissakes. I look like the Goodyear blimp."

"Nevertheless, Lockwood couldn't take his eyes off you."

"Husband dear, I do believe you're jealous." Lee smiled and reached for my left hand, lacing her fingers through mine. "But you're wrong about his suspicions. Lockwood's just being thorough."

"Maybe. But he's also being a cop. Did you notice how he carefully rationed out the information?"

"I thought he was being very straightforward." Lee braked for the traffic signal at the corner of First Avenue and East Thirty-eighth Street.

"You would." I glared at the throng of pedestrians in the crosswalk. With abrupt realization, I asked, "Why are you still heading north?"

"I thought we were going to the apartment."

"What about lunch?" The enticing smells at Carmine's had excited my taste buds, and I realized I was suddenly hungry.

"All right," Lee said. "How about a late lunch in Chinatown?"

"Chinatown?" I grumbled. "I don't want to go to China-town."

"Fine." Lee lightly drummed her open palms against the steering wheel. "You pick the place then."

With sudden inspiration, I answered boldly, "Eleventh and Broadway."

"Now, Kyle—"

"Look, I just want to see the scene of the crime."

"Can't you leave the investigation to the police?" Lee tapped the horn to alert the daydreaming driver in the car ahead of us that the light had changed.

"Not when my life's on the line."

"Oh, all right, I give up. But you'll have to direct me. I'm not too sure how to get there from here."

I laughed. "Don't play dumb with me. You know this town

better than I do. Just take a left up here on Forty-second, and we'll head back south on Second Avenue."

My familiarity with Manhattan geography resulted primarily from the location of bookstores. For instance, I knew Midtown because that's where Otto Penzler's Mysterious Book Shop resided, as well as all the major chain stores on Fifth Avenue; the Upper West Side offered Murder Ink, the Upper East Side had the Black Orchid, the Village housed Partners & Crime, and the Lower East Side sported the Strand—the world's largest book emporium—which, if I remembered correctly, was just around the corner from Eleventh and Broadway. And not far from where gentleman burglar Bernard G. Rhodenbarr—or Bernie to his millions of fans—operates his secondhand bookstore. The Mansard Building had to be within that general vicinity.

"We can go to Chinatown afterward," I added as an incentive.

"Oh, you're so magnanimous," Lee said sarcastically. But she was smiling.

"There!" A few minutes later, after several skillful driving maneuvers, Lee turned off Eleventh and cautiously threaded the Land Rover through a slender opening between a line of double-parked cars and delivery vans occupying both sides of the street. I pointed to a structure mid-block. "There! That one says Mansard Building." The words had been chiseled into the stone above the entrance.

"Parking's going to be a problem," Lee said.

I laughed. "Surely not for the Teflon ticket queen of New York."

"Well, believe it. Because right now I don't even see an illegal space." She whistled. "I've never seen such a mess. What's going on? A paramilitary convention or something?"

Lee drove another block and a half before she finally

located enough room to maneuver the Land Rover next to the curb. She barely grazed the fire hydrant.

"You're asking for it again," I said as we stepped onto the sidewalk.

"Didn't you know? I live a charmed life. Though let's just hope there's not a fire in the next five minutes."

"Five minutes? Is that all the time you're giving me?"

"Should be more than ample."

"Now who's being magnanimous?"

She ignored me. "Just what are you hoping to accomplish with this visit anyway?"

"I don't know, but I can't just leave it in the hands of the police. I've got to do everything I can to prove my innocence."

"I think you're wrong about Lockwood."

I laughed. "You think he told us everything, huh? Just laid it all out for us as if we were his fellow investigators?"

Lee nodded her head. "Yes, as a matter of fact, I do. He gave us a lot of information, certainly more than he had to."

"He only told us what he wanted us to know," I said smugly.

"What makes you say that?"

I stared at her. "Why didn't he consider the possibility of a mugging? In this neighborhood, I'd think that would top the list."

"Well—"

"Or why was he so quick to believe the Stokes Moran identification was bogus?"

"You persuaded him—"

"Hah!" I cut her off in mid-sentence and provided the answer myself. "I'll tell you why. It's because he knows more than he's saying."

"Kyle, you don't know that."

"Yes, I do," I said. "And I'm about to do something about it."

The dusty red-brick Mansard Building—a throwback to the architecture of another time—loomed ahead on our right. Candy wrappers and cigarette butts littered the entrance. One homeless person lay curled into a blanket on the adjacent sidewalk while another sat on the steps leading up to the front doors. At our approach, the squatter asked for a quarter. Lee and I both ignored his request.

"I don't like this place," Lee said once we were inside. I didn't blame her. The lobby was dark, the tile floor was cracked and dirty, and the air smelled suspiciously foul. I didn't even want to speculate on what lethal combination created that fetid odor. "Let's get out of here," she said.

"You gave me five minutes," I reminded her. "You can wait outside if you like."

Lee looked back over her shoulder. "Not on your life."

"Then follow me." I reached for her hand. "And try to be quiet."

On the far wall, a faded green sign with black lettering indicated that there was an elevator to the left. I turned in that direction but bypassed the single elevator door. Ahead, the corridor turned again, this time to the right.

"Where are you going?" Lee whispered.

"Lockwood said the police had to break out a ground-floor window to get to the body. I want to locate that window."

"Why?"

I let the question go unanswered. Finally, another turn to the right revealed a bank of blacked-out windows on the left side of the corridor. Fresh air filtered through the last one in the row where several strips of yellow POLICE LINE DO NOT CROSS tape crisscrossed the broken panes and splintered wood. Since first access is usually easiest, I assumed the police must have arrived from the opposite direction.

Lee rushed to the window, pressed her face against the tape, and swallowed a huge intake of air. "I can breathe again."

I looked past the flimsy barrier at the area beyond. At one time, probably when the building had first been constructed, the ground surface had been paved over with concrete. Now, grass and weeds sprouted through the numerous chips in the wrecked cement. Aluminum cans, paper plates, newspaper circulars, and other assorted garbage clustered against the base of the four walls.

Lee had been right. There was nothing here of apparent significance, no sign of violence or death, not even any telltale bloodstains. So Lockwood was probably right when he had concluded that the man had been killed elsewhere and then brought here. But why? Why would the murderer take that kind of risk? I had the certain conviction that the answer, if I could find it, would lead me to the mysterious killer.

I pondered the riddle until Lee impatiently announced, "Your five minutes are up!"

"All right," I said. "Let's go."

We retraced our labyrinthine route and returned to the lobby. Lee led the way out the door and down the steps. Suddenly I stopped.

Lee turned back to me. "Now what?"

The squatter had left, perhaps for more generous pastures, but the inhabitant of the blanket remained, except she—I surmised it was a woman, despite all the grime and layers of clothing—now leaned propped sideways against the building's outside wall. She had one end of a frayed rope tied around her left foot while the other end stretched to a wire grocery cart piled to overflowing with bags and bundles.

"Excuse me," I said, kneeling beside the woman.

Her eyes were closed, but she held a lighted cigarette between her lips.

"Kyle, what are you doing?" Lee demanded.

I nudged the woman's shoulder with my hand. Her eyelids fluttered open.

"Are you crazy?" Lee hissed in my ear.

"Lemme alone." The woman retreated into the blanket until only her face was visible. Then she added, "Whaddaya want?"

I smiled. "Have you been here long?"

"Yeah, since the Roosevelt administration." At least she had a sense of humor, warped though it was.

The woman tucked the blanket more firmly under her chin. "This is my place," she said with a proprietary tone in her voice.

I studied her withered face. Dirt streaked her cheeks and chin, her eyes appeared rheumy and bloodshot, and her teeth—the few that she still retained—were black and rotted. Her stringy hair was a blotchy gray and matted against her scalp. I judged her age at somewhere between fifty and eternity. Maybe she had been here since the Roosevelt administration, after all. And not necessarily FDR's.

"Don' nobody mess wimme," she warned.

"Did you see anything this morning?" I persisted. "Before the police got here?"

She gave me a broken-toothed smile. "Name's Amy. Call me Amy."

I repeated my question. "Did you see anything this morning, Amy?"

"Wazzit's worth to ya?"

I patted my pockets, immediately realizing that Lockwood had not returned my money clip. The sly devil, I decided, he had kept it on purpose. I turned to Lee. "Do you have any cash?" I asked.

"Kyle, are you insane? Dickering with a street person? You can't trust a word she says. She's just leading you on so you'll give her money for booze. Anyway, you know I only use credit cards."

"I'll take plastic," said Amy, struggling to rise to her knees.

"I'll just bet you will." Lee gave me a disapproving stare. "Kyle, this is lunacy."

"I'll take your shoes," Amy countered.

"What?" Lee's face reddened. "Like hell you will."

"Not yours, honey. His."

"Kyle—"

"Lee, why don't you go get the car. Let me handle this."

"But—"

"Go on. I'll be all right."

"It's your funeral." Lee spiraled around on her heels and stormed off down the sidewalk. I slipped off my loafers and extended them toward Amy. As she reached forward, I raised the Guccis above her grasp.

"Did you see anything?" I said gruffly.

"Mebbe. First the shoes."

I lowered my hands. Like a scavenger crab, Amy greedily grabbed the prize, then quickly stuffed the shoes under the blanket.

"Were three of 'em."

"Three men?"

She nodded.

"What time was this?" I asked.

"Haw, I ain't no clock." She spat out the dead cigarette. "Socks."

"Socks?" At first I didn't understand what she was saying, then I realized she wanted my socks in exchange for another answer. She waited expectantly while I peeled off my argyles.

"'Fore light."

"Before sunrise. Is that what you're telling me?"

Again she nodded.

Sometime before seven-thirty A.M., I concluded. In another two weeks, the annual switch to standard time would push back the dawn to around six-thirty. But not yet, not today. Sometime before seven-thirty was the best I could do. That only improved the police timetable by a half hour, not much of a victory.

"Can you tell me anything about these three men?" I persisted.

Amy gawked at me. "Shirt," she said.

"No way." I was already standing barefooted in the middle of a busy New York City sidewalk, and I wasn't about to bare my chest. I shook my head.

"Shirt," she repeated.

I met her vacant gaze. She'd even give Buddha a run for his money.

"Oh, hell," I said after a minute, unbuttoning my Armani. "Here." I threw her the shirt. It instantly disappeared underneath the blanket.

"Warn't drunk," she said. "The middle un. Other two were a-holdin' him up."

"How do you know he wasn't drunk?"

"Haw," she cawed like a crow. "I oughta know daid when I sees it." Then she added more softly, "I'se seen it enuf."

I could easily visualize the scene. One man on each side of the dead man, holding him up and propelling him forward. To any curious eyes, it would appear that the poor sot had just had a little too much to drink and that his considerate friends were kindly taking him home. Such a performance had been successfully staged in countless books and movies. Why not in real life as well?

"Anything else?" I asked with dread.

She nodded. "Pants," she said.

"No!" I shook my head adamantly. "Absolutely not."

Amy sat as immobile and trancelike as the Sphinx. Oh, what the hell, I decided as I unbuckled my belt and peeled the Calvin Kleins down my legs and off my ankles. I dangled the jeans in front of her face, and she quickly snatched them away.

"Well?" I prodded. Even though the October sunlight still

bounced brilliantly off the sidewalk, there was a definite chill to the air. My bare skin tightened against the cool.

"Nutter man in the car," Amy answered.

"Car? You mean you saw the car?"

She nodded.

"Didn't they see you?"

"'Ems never pay me no mind," she said.

I understood. Street people had become merely another anonymous part of the big city background, no more remarkable than a stray dog or cat. And usually just as silent. I suspected the killers had not even noticed Amy. That reprehensible disregard, that social invisibility, had probably saved her life.

"Could you identify the men?"

She shook her head.

"Or the car?"

She grinned. "Shorts."

"No!" I shouted. "No way! Forget it!"

Standing on the sidewalk in my Jockeys, I'd already endured the curious stares and snickers of a couple of pedestrians. Stripping down to the buff was completely out of the question. But then, Amy's information had so far proved valuable.

She remained mute. I decided to argue my case.

"Why would you possibly want my shorts?" I appealed in desperation.

"Caw, mister. I ain't seen a good-lookin' guy like you in twenty year. Ya think I'm gonna pass up this here opernoonity?"

I shook my head. I just couldn't do it. Just to this point, I knew Lee would pitch a fit over the public striptease.

"I'm sorry," I told her. "You've already gotten all the thrills you're going to get at my expense. The shorts stay on."

Amy looked me over appraisingly, wondering, I suppose, just how resolute was I in my refusal. Her eyes now sparkled with energy, resurrected from their previous lackadaisical state by this contest of wills. Under her scrutiny, I suddenly felt shorter than my six feet and heavier than my hundred and fifty pounds. Further insecurities I forced from my mind.

"All right," I said irritably. "You've had your fun. The game is over. Now what about the car?"

Amy shrugged with a sigh, obviously concluding that I couldn't be bullied any further. "Big sedan," she said. "Dark."

"Model? Make?"

She shook her head.

"Did you get the license number?"

"Naw."

"Now don't tell me I peeled all the way down to my skivvies for nothing. I thought you knew something that I could use." What was keeping Lee? I focused my attention on Amy and pretended ignorance of the crowd that was forming on the sidewalk. I definitely didn't hear their hoots and whistles.

"Gummint," she said.

Gummint? What did she mean by gummint? I thought for a minute. "Are you saying government? It was a government car?"

Amy nodded. I heard brakes squeal.

"Kyle, are you out of your mind?" Lee shouted, standing halfway above the Land Rover's sunroof. "What happened to your clothes?"

I darted through the crowd, ignoring the raucous laughter, slapping away a couple of overtly inquisitive hands, ran out into the street, my feet barely touching the pavement, and leaped into the Land Rover.

"Kyle, what in the world were you thinking?" Lee demanded in a loud, shocked voice that could easily have been heard all the way down in Battery Park. "Are you nuts?

Stripping down to your underwear in the middle of a New York City street?"

"Don't ask stupid questions," I yelled at my wife, wedging myself protectively between the seat and the floorboard. "Just burn rubber."

Fortunately, my wife didn't need to be told twice.

CHAPTER **SEVEN**

*"The author
makes
an impassioned plea
for both ethnic understanding
as well as
cultural diversity."*

—Stokes Moran,
on Manuel Ramos's *The Ballad of Rocky Ruiz*

"*I* have to grant you one thing," Lee said. "You gave a whole new meaning to the term jaywalking."

"Very funny," I answered as I struggled into the running outfit Lee had just purchased in a thrift store on East Fourth Street. It had taken her three tries before she had found a merchant who accepted credit cards, and I had been forced to be satisfied with whatever clothing she selected. After all, I wasn't exactly in a position to be choosy.

"These shoes are too tight," I complained as I tied the laces on the sneakers.

"Just be grateful you have something to wear at all," Lee said.

"It's all Lockwood's fault," I said irritably. "If he hadn't kept my money clip—intentionally, I might add—then I

wouldn't have had to surrender my clothes to that old letch."
I sat back against the seat. "Remind me to thank him properly someday."

"As well as get back your money clip, and by the way,
we're stopping at the next automatic teller machine we come
to. Get you some cash in your pockets so you won't ever be
tempted to repeat this folly again."

"Good idea," I said, straightening up in the seat. "All
right, I'm suitably attired once again, though I'm sure that in
this outfit I won't make any of this year's best-dressed lists.
What now?"

"Have you forgotten? You promised me a late lunch in
Chinatown."

"You can't still be serious. After what I've just been
through, all I want to do is go home."

"I'm not letting you off that easy. Besides, you owe me."

"It's too late for a late lunch."

"Then I'll settle for an early dinner. Either way, we're
going to Chinatown. I'm starved."

The Canton Palace sat squarely on Canal Street, in the geographic heart of New York City's Chinatown, the largest metropolitan concentration of Chinese inhabitants this side of
Shanghai. Once again, Lee parked the Land Rover in an illegal zone. This time I made no comment.

"I hope the restaurant's not crowded," Lee said dubiously.

"At this hour?" I glanced at my watch. It was only four-
thirty.

"But look at all those people."

It was true. Twenty to thirty Chinese thronged around the
entrance to the Canton Palace. As we edged closer, we discovered the reason.

Two Chinese men carried homemade signs, one decrying
that "Charlie Chan Is Bad" and another that demanded

"Down with Charlie Chan." A Chinese woman sat at a nearby table draped with a paper invitation to "Register Your Protest Against the Evil Chan."

"I can't believe this," I said with total consternation. "This is all wrong. America loves Charlie Chan. I love Charlie Chan."

"Kyle, don't make a scene."

"I'm not going to make a scene. I just want to find out what this is all about."

"Isn't it obvious?"

"Excuse me." I addressed the woman behind the table. "Can you explain what's going on here?"

"Charlie Chan gives all Chinese people a bad name," she said. "Will you sign the petition?"

I could have argued that Charlie Chan was a brilliant detective, that he outsmarted even the world's master criminals. But I decided not to wage the useless war. She already had her mind made up.

I started to walk away. The woman thrust a sheet of paper toward me and repeated, "Sign the petition."

I shook my head. Without a word between us, I guided Lee into the restaurant.

"I'm proud of you." Lee finally spoke as we followed the hostess up the stairs.

"Debating the issue wouldn't have done any good," I said sadly. "Those people already had their minds made up."

Once we were seated, Lee informed the hostess that we would have dim sum. The waitress answered that it was too late for a tea lunch. Lee frowned, then proceeded to order duck chow fun, bean curd family style, and Chinese broccoli. For two.

"All right with you?" she asked me in a voice that held almost a challenge.

"Fine," I said. "I'm not hungry anyway." The street protest had taken my mind completely off food.

As we waited for the order to arrive, I pondered the potential implications of what I had just witnessed outside.

Right now, I wasn't the only one in big trouble. So was my old friend Charlie Chan.

No more Charlie Chan? The idea was inconceivable. The most popular Oriental sleuth of all time appeared to be in danger of imminent annihilation. Was this but the latest manifestation of political correctness?

I attempted to analyze the conflict. To be fair, I could somewhat understand how activist groups—such as those people just now out on Canal Street—might justifiably claim that the character of Charlie Chan was as demeaning to Chinese-Americans as Amos and Andy had been to African-Americans. But I also felt they were oversimplifying the problem.

Charlie Chan wasn't their enemy; Hollywood was.

While I have always enjoyed those classic black-and-white B movies from Tinseltown's heyday, I must admit that the producers had often seemed more intent on transforming Charlie into a broad comedic box office draw than in maintaining his literary credibility.

As mystery readers well know, Charlie Chan came across much better in the books. Author Earl Derr Biggers was a lifelong student of Chinese history and culture, and he was also keenly aware and respectful of ethnic sensitivities and sensibilities. In the Biggers novels, Charlie Chan was a far cry from the overblown caricature seen on the screen. Plus, it must be remembered that the stories are more than sixty years old, and that certain attitudes and prejudices are simply reflective of the time in which they were written. That's called history.

As fate would have it, I had recently reread one of Charlie Chan's most famous cases—the 1932 novel *Keeper of the Keys*. In that book, Charlie Chan was more of an intellect, more of a gentleman, and more of a diplomat than all the other characters combined. He was both moral instructor and compassionate friend, and he proudly stood head and shoulders above the story's mere mortals. Charlie Chan had been magnificent, very much the equal of Hercule Poirot, Ellery Queen, Nero Wolfe, and even Sherlock Holmes.

How could such a superhuman performer be judged objectionable?

Keeper of the Keys is a classic in the best sense of the word. The novel contains all the hallmarks of great mystery fiction—a challenging puzzle that only the great detective can solve, an explosive cast of characters to confuse and confound the intrepid sleuth, and a dazzling setting that is both wild and exotic. Earl Derr Biggers was a true original. And so was his creation.

Today's standards should not be required for yesterday's heroes, otherwise there'd be no heroes left. Despite all the righteous chest-beating of his misguided detractors, it's time to let Charlie Chan rest in peace.

"Kyle, you haven't said a word in more than ten minutes," Lee said. "Don't you like the food?"

I looked down at my plate. I hadn't even been aware the food had been served, yet obviously I had consumed a reasonable portion of it already, but without the slightest memory of taste or texture.

"It's fine," I assured my wife. "I was just thinking about something."

"I bet I can guess what." Lee reached across the table and gently covered my hand with hers. "Don't let it worry you. The police will get to the bottom of it."

I smiled. For once, my wife's usually miraculous mind-reading wizardry had failed her. "Thanks."

"By the way, you haven't told me yet what the bag lady said. Was the information worth the embarrassment?" She grinned.

I felt my face reddening. "Uh-huh."

Lee laughed, dabbing her napkin against the corner of her mouth. "Then stop your blushing and tell me all about it."

I summarized for Lee the facts that I had extracted from Amy, attempting to assemble them in some sort of rational and logical order.

"You believe her?"

I nodded. "Yes, I do. I don't see any reason why she'd lie to me."

"To get your shorts, for one thing."

"Am I going to hear about this for the rest of my life?" I asked sarcastically.

"Probably." She smiled. "Are you sure she said it was a government car?"

"Absolutely."

"How would she know it was a government car?"

"I don't know."

"But you think it's credible." Lee paused. "Kyle, it just doesn't make any sense."

"I agree, and I've been saying that from the beginning. This whole doggone mess doesn't make any sense." The chopsticks accidentally slipped from my fingers, clattering as they fell into my plate, splattering the sweet-and-sour sauce onto the tablecloth. I quickly rubbed at the stain with my napkin.

"You're making a mess," Lee said sternly. "Here. Why don't you try this lemon?"

My wife's suggestion didn't work either. Finally, in defeat, I dropped my napkin over the offending stain, hiding it from sight. Let's hope the Canton Palace knew a good Chinese laundry.

"Let's get out of here," I said, pushing my chair back from the table.

"But I haven't had dessert."

"We can pick up some frozen yogurt on the way to your place."

Lee hurriedly grabbed her handbag and followed me to

the captain's station. She handed the attendant a credit card, and two minutes later we were once again standing on the sidewalk. The Charlie Chan bashers were nowhere to be seen, but the Land Rover was just as we had left it, no ticket or tow in sight.

"Do you seriously believe government officials had anything to do with this murder?" Lee asked as she unlocked the car door.

"It could have been some kind of undercover operation gone wrong," I suggested, sliding into the passenger seat. "Or a drug deal gone bad."

"Then why the Stokes Moran ID?" Lee shook her head. "I just can't see the FBI or some other government agency planting false identification on a dead man just to implicate you. For what possible reason? No, it makes more sense that the guy was in the process of setting you up for some sort of shakedown."

"Maybe it will all come clear eventually," I said.

"I hope so. I'm just afraid you're putting too much faith in what that bag lady told you. She could have been making the whole thing up and heading you down the proverbial garden path, when you should be focusing your attention elsewhere."

I carefully considered what Lee had said as she pulled the Land Rover out into the early evening traffic. Was Amy a reliable witness? Could her information be trusted? I admit I too had problems coming up with a believable scenario that would explain government involvement. DEA? CIA? INS? IRS? The myriad agencies and variations were limitless, yet not one made a lick of sense.

I was back at square one. Exactly nowhere. I was frustrated, impotent, more confused than ever.

And, as far as Lockwood was concerned, still the prime suspect.

CHAPTER **EIGHT**

*"But
the persistent detective
won't
abandon the scent,
no matter
how cold the trail gets."*

—Stokes Moran,
on Nancy Baker Jacobs's *The Turquoise Tattoo*

"*K*yle, we've got to have food," Lee insisted.

"I'm too tired to fool with grocery shopping right now."

Lee shook her head. "I haven't been to the apartment in weeks. Believe me when I say the cupboard is bare."

"Well, we just ate. Surely we can survive until tomorrow."

"You always want coffee when you first get up in the morning."

"I can wait."

"Well, I can't," Lee persisted. "While we're still out, we might as well pick up at least a few items. It'll be a lot easier if we just get the shopping over and done with, and quit arguing about it."

I decided to abandon my objections; I knew I had no chance of winning the argument anyway.

We covered the next few blocks in silence. More than likely, given her present preoccupation with food, Lee was currently composing in her head a grocery want list while I, on the other hand, continued to concentrate my thoughts on the man in the morgue.

I doubted that I'd be able to make any headway at all on the case until I knew the identity of the dead man. If nothing else, my mystery reading had taught me that you have to know the who before you can figure out the why. And right now, the reason for his death—and whether or not I might be a target—didn't seem as crucial as putting a name to the body.

Obviously, he hadn't existed in a vacuum. No one in this world does. Even Robinson Crusoe had his Friday. The man had been somebody's son, likely even somebody's husband or boyfriend. He might even be somebody's father. He probably had friends, possibly co-workers, which meant also an employer. Somebody would miss him, perhaps even come looking for him. Somebody knew who he was, and at the moment I wished that I was that somebody.

Somebody somewhere knew who the man was. Or I should say is. Because more than likely it wasn't yet known to the people in his life that he was dead. Unless one of them killed him. Which, after all, seemed to be the most reasonable solution.

Because victims and their killers normally know each other, both in real life and in fiction. Of course, anonymity may exist in incidents of serial killings and drive-by shootings and random murders. But even in those cases, unexpected and unforeseen links can oftentimes be established to connect and ultimately trap the killer. Most frequently, however, the murderer is a member of the victim's daily circle—family member, friend, or acquaintance. That's why, if I could somehow identify the man in the morgue, I might also be able, with a lot of luck, to identify the person who put him there.

It all sounded like some lurid thriller from the 1930s—
The Corpse Had No Name. Envisioning that title gave me the
shivers.

"Kyle, we're here." Lee's abrupt announcement brought
me crashing back to the present. I recognized the store. It
was located just around the corner from her building. She
had once again pulled in next to the curb, in another clearly
marked tow-away zone.

"Lee, why don't we park in the underground garage of
your building? You pay a fortune for your monthly space, and
you hardly ever use it anymore," I reminded her. "There's
hardly any difference in the distance, maybe a few extra steps
is all."

"This will be fine," she said, killing the engine, depositing the car keys into her handbag, and opening her door.
"We'll only be a minute."

"Why don't I just wait here?"

"Kyle, I'll need your help. Especially when it comes to
carrying the sacks."

Sacks?

"This is going to be a long process, isn't it?" I predicted.

In lieu of an answer, Lee slid off the seat and slammed her
door behind her.

I meekly followed my wife into the market.

Thirty minutes later we had progressed no farther than midway down the second aisle, and the shopping cart was
already full.

"Are you planning on feeding an army?" I asked Lee
irritably.

It's no wonder my mind drifted back to the bogus Stokes
Moran. Not only was he known by somebody, he had clearly
existed somewhere. In addition to establishing the man's
identity, I felt that the somewhere could also be a most deci-

sive factor. Whether he turned out to be a native New Yorker, or a tourist in from Florida, or a businessman on a trip from California, his previous geographic inhabitation could prove important.

Or he could have been an illegal immigrant, an undocumented alien, a foreigner with no ties to this country. A person with that kind of background might be a target for blackmail or coercion. Or worse.

I felt as if I were back in my college Journalism 101 class, wrangling once again with the imponderable who, what, when, where, and why.

Both the what—the manner of death—and the when—the time of death—would be officially determined by the coroner. But unless something totally unexpected showed up in the ME's final report, those were two areas that seemed, at least for the moment, fairly well answered—the man had been knifed sometime last night or early this morning.

So I was left with three big "W's" to consider. The where—not so much where the body was found but more where he had been killed and where he had lived. The who— of course, if I knew who had killed him, the case would be over and I would be out of jeopardy. No, for my fledgling detective efforts, more the who that he had been, the man himself. And the why—why had the man been killed, easily the most essential but probably the last question that would be resolved.

"What do you think about pancakes?"

Lee and I were now standing in front of the packaged mixes section. I shook my head in disbelief.

"Don't you think you have enough stuff?"

"Okay," she said. "No pancakes."

However, Lee did amazingly manage to add a couple of more items to the haul en route to the checkout counter. After the final bill had been computed, Lee handed over a credit card.

"Oh," she added in dismay, "I forgot the frozen yogurt. Is

it too late?" she asked the checker. "No? Then, Kyle, will you be a sweetie and get us two cups from the machine?"

She pointed out the location, and as I grudgingly walked toward the far corner, Lee called after me, "Be sure to get the large size. With sprinkles."

Once I stowed the grocery bags in the back of the Land Rover, the short ride to the apartment building, by way of a Chase Manhattan ATM on the corner, where Lee withdrew fifty dollars, took less than five minutes.

"You've been awfully quiet," Lee said as she pulled into the opening to the underground garage. "Where's Leonard?" She honked the horn, but the usual attendant was nowhere in sight. "Oh well, I'll park it myself." She steered the Land Rover down the steep ramp. "Okay, so tell me why you're suddenly so quiet."

"Just thinking."

"About what?"

For one thing, about the three teenaged boys I'd just spotted over next to a white Mercedes, one of whom was swinging at an imaginary baseball with a very real baseball bat. Maybe that explained what had happened to Leonard.

"Come on, Lee," I said once she had eased the Land Rover into the narrow parking space. "Let's get the groceries out fast."

"Kyle, it's going to take at least two trips for both of us."

I stood at the back of the car, the trunk door already opened. "I'll double up," I said, grabbing as many sacks as I could manage.

"Let me see. There should be a pushcart around here someplace." Lee headed toward the access stairway.

I finally managed to get the three grocery bags hefted up into my arms. Then I staggered after Lee, always keeping those three boys in some part of my vision.

"Really, Kyle," Lee said, emerging from a door marked LAUNDRY. "You'll kill yourself." In front of her, she pushed a supermarket cart, one wheel of which appeared to be locked in place.

"It's either me or them," I whispered, nodding toward the three boys to my left. Lee followed my gaze.

"Is that what's got you spooked?" she asked with a laugh. "Those are the Martin kids from the fourth floor."

"Oh." I dropped the sacks into the wire basket.

"Appearances can be deceiving," Lee reminded me. "Not everything turns out to be the way it looks."

Was she talking about the boys—who quite clearly on second look seemed a lot less threatening, almost benign—or my current predicament with the police?

Lee could be right, I considered as I finished loading the rest of the groceries into the rickety reject from an ancient A&P. Maybe Lockwood didn't have me pegged as his most likely fella, after all.

I hadn't even made it halfway to the elevator before I dismissed that possibility entirely. No, I was a patsy made in police heaven. It didn't take a Hercule Poirot with his little gray cells to see that Lockwood saw me as an early Christmas present, and he had me all but gift-wrapped and delivered. To Sing Sing no less.

As Lee and I rode up in the elevator, the shopping cart jammed between us, I decided that Lockwood should best forget about Santa Claus. At least for this year.

I wasn't going down without a fight.

CHAPTER NINE

"The author
presents the conflicts
without judgment,
without undue prejudice,
outlining the pros and cons
on both sides."

—Stokes Moran,
on Margaret Maron's *Shooting at Loons*

" *K*yle, I thought you were going to call Nolan."

"I tried, but the line was busy."

Lee and I had unlocked the door to her apartment just five minutes earlier, time enough for my wife to bewail the stuffy atmosphere and bemoan the dust that had accumulated on the furnishings in the past month. Lee normally had a cleaning lady come in once a week, but the woman's husband had died in late September and my wife had not pressed the woman on when she would return to work. Consequently, the rooms had not been aired in several weeks. Of course, the doorman came up every few days to water the plants. But, since even that generously compensated chore wasn't in his regular job description, Marco never volunteered for anything more than that.

In the elevator, I had offered to help Lee put away the groceries once we arrived, but Lee told me in no uncertain terms that it was her kitchen, she knew where everything belonged, and I would just get in her way. So, taking only the barest amount of time needed to first drop her handbag on the living room sofa and then hurriedly stash the grocery items that required immediate freezing or refrigeration, Lee had transformed herself into a zealot housekeeper, scurrying around throwing open all the windows. Once she had the fresh outside air infusing new life into the stale interior, she then turned into a broom jockey riding herd on all wayward dust bunnies, followed closely by a determined dustbuster on a demented Pledge patrol.

I grew exhausted just watching my wife's tornadic efforts in the living room, so I retreated into the bedroom, where I sorted through Lee's closet for the old clothes I'd left there a few months ago, back when both Lee and I were still using the apartment as a semi-regular residence. Jammed into one side of the overhead shelf, I found a pullover cardigan sweater and a pair of Levi's. They both smelled a little musty, but they proved much more comfortable than the thrift store outfit I'd been wearing. However, the real heaven, at least for my feet, was found in the suede loafers I discovered on the closet floor.

When I returned to the living room, Lee never even remarked on my change of clothing. No wonder, then, that she had also failed to notice my unsuccessful attempt to reach Nolan. She was too preoccupied playing Mrs. Clean.

"Will you please let that go?" I said irritably, snapping on the arc lamp over the sofa.

"I've got to get this place straightened up. It's a mess."

I sat down on the sofa. "Right now, it's another mess entirely I'm concerned about."

"Kyle, stop worrying," she said, carefully polishing a carved jade figurine, then replacing it gingerly back in the precise center of the table. "The police will handle it."

"That's exactly what I'm afraid of." I grabbed her hand as it swept within my reach. "Now will you sit down so we can talk this out. I've been doing some thinking."

Lee laughed and fell against me on the sofa. "All right," she said as she nestled under my outstretched arm, "talk."

"We've got to simplify what we can," I began. "It's all too confused."

"Agreed," she murmured, her jaw moving against my chest. "How do we do that?"

"First, it's not so important that we figure out who did it, but who it was done to."

"Identify the dead man?"

"Right, and we start with the premise that he is not Stokes Moran."

"That's fairly obvious."

I nodded, the tip of my chin nudging against her skull. "But, if by some miracle it turns out his real name is Stokes Moran, I'm in the clear. The police will just chalk it up as a bizarre mix-up. But I don't think that's the case, although somewhere in this big wide world there probably is somebody other than me who goes by the name of Stokes Moran."

"But not him?"

"No. The coincidence is just too great. It's not like the Bob Smith society where you have a name so common that thousands of men share it. I'd be surprised if there are more than two or three Stokes Morans in the entire universe."

"One is enough for me." Lee nuzzled my ear.

"Will you stop!" I pulled my arm from around her shoulders and let it drop to my lap. "I'm trying to be serious here."

"I know, darling. I'll be good."

"So, if the dead man is not Stokes Moran, and we both admit that's not likely, then who is he? As I see it, that's the real sixty-four-thousand-dollar question."

"Won't the police find that out?"

"Maybe. But until they do, I'm still bachelor number one

in their murderers' dating game. And, believe me, I don't like the hot seat one bit."

"Then how do we go about finding out who the dead man was?" Lee asked. "The last time I looked, we didn't have the least thing to go on."

"We saw him, remember?"

Lee frowned. "Just for an instant. That's not going to get us anywhere."

"I wouldn't be too sure. What do you remember about him?"

Lee concentrated, a vacant gaze transfixing her eyes. "Well, he was a big man, I suppose. Probably six-two, two hundred twenty pounds."

"But not fat?"

"No, he looked"—she struggled for the best description—"muscular."

"Good," I said with relief. "That's the impression I had as well."

"And he had dark hair," she added.

I shook my head. "Not dark. Black."

Lee frowned. "What's the difference?"

"Perhaps nothing." I paused, folding my arms across my chest. "What else?"

"I don't know. Height, weight, color of hair." Lee shrugged. "That's all I noticed. Except," she said offhandedly, "he was white."

"Not white." I edged closer to her.

"Of course he was white. You're not trying to tell me he was as black as his hair, are you?"

"No, of course not. But he wasn't exactly white, was he?" I asked excitedly.

Scowling, Lee gave me a puzzled look. "What are you getting at?"

"His skin. How would you describe his skin?"

"Tanned?"

I shook my head.

"Swarthy?"

I nodded eagerly. "Olive-complected?" I asked.

"I suppose."

"Southern European?"

"Kyle, I don't know where you're heading, but we're not going to be able to determine his country of origin. That's just too ridiculous."

I stood up. "Just bear with me for a minute, okay? We have a man who is powerfully built, physically fit, possibly Greek or Italian."

Lee frowned again. "He could just as easily be one hundred percent American, and you know that. Or he could be from a thousand other spots in the world. You're making too big of a jump."

I waved away her objections. "Forget all that. Close your eyes and think back to the precise moment you saw the body. In that fleeting instant, what nationality would you assign him to?"

Lee sighed. "Kyle, this is a waste of time. Oh, all right." She closed her eyes for a second, then said, "Italian, I suppose."

"Right," I shouted with eager anticipation. "Now put it all together—large powerful Italian. What does that suggest to you?"

"Sylvester Stallone."

I frowned in irritation. "Come on, stop playing around," I chided. "This is serious."

Lee shook her head. "Kyle, I know where you're heading, and this is not at all like you. It's prejudicial." My wife stood up and walked toward the window. Then she turned and faced me, her cheeks glowing red. "You get into a little bit of trouble, and what's the first thing you do? You fall back on stereotypes, that's what."

"Just answer me. What do those traits suggest?"

"The mob, of course." Lee said angrily. "That's what you want me to say, isn't it?"

"Exactly. And once you think about it, it all begins to make sense."

"I don't see how."

"The forged documents. The Mafia wouldn't have any trouble manufacturing those."

"Neither would Office Depot."

I ignored the barbed remark.

"It also eliminates the time problem. Those documents weren't part of some last-minute effort to disguise the identity of the body. No, those cards had been prepared long before." I stopped, then added with certainty, "Yes, it's definitely the money they're after. The billion or so dollars that I'm about to inherit." I paced the floor, thinking out loud. "The mob was in the process of setting up some scam—extortion, probably— maybe even impersonation."

"May I remind you, Mr. Malachi," Lee interrupted with overt sarcasm, "that the dead man didn't look a thing like you."

I thought for a moment, then suggested, "But maybe the killer did. Yes, I can see it now. The killer and the dead man were partners. They had devised this plan where the killer would impersonate me. Then, for some reason, they had a falling-out and—"

Lee interrupted. "That makes no sense at all. If someone was going to impersonate you in order to get the money, wouldn't he attempt to impersonate Kyle Malachi instead? After all, Stokes Moran has no claim to the inheritance."

I cupped my chin in my hand and considered her objection seriously.

"Good point," I answered. "Okay, then it wasn't going to be an impersonation."

"Kyle, this is totally absurd. You're leaping to all sorts of unfounded conclusions. This isn't detective work, it's mindless speculation. You're not solving anything."

"No, no, no . . . just hear me out, okay?" I paused, trying

to gather my wild thoughts into a presentable pattern that would prove convincing to Lee. "The whole scheme revolved around Stokes Moran. These people, whoever they were, were in the process of building some sort of incriminating case against Stokes Moran so that I'd have no choice but to pay blackmail to keep it quiet. But, without knowing it, I beat them to the punch. When I put Moran's death notice in the paper, their whole plan fell apart. Then, out of frustration, they must have fought and—oh my God." I stopped dead in my tracks. "For all intents and purposes, I suppose I'm responsible for the man's death. I'm the murderer after all."

"Kyle, that's the biggest load of crap I've ever heard."

"I don't think it's so far-fetched."

Lee shook her head decisively. "Then you haven't been listening to yourself. You've let your imagination run wild. For all we know, the man's death resulted from a simple drug deal gone bad. In that neighborhood, those type killings happen all the time." Lee patted me on the back. "Now, do something useful. Call Nolan and get the animals taken care of."

"I didn't think I was all that off base," I said defensively, picking up the phone and punching the redial button.

"It was a total waste of time and didn't solve a thing."

"Well, at least we agreed that the man wasn't Stokes Moran." In my ear, the fifth ring triggered Nolan's answering machine.

Lee laughed. "That's the only thing. And we had effectively established that point well before you lost your senses."

"There must be something we can do." Through the phone, I heard Nolan's recorded voice.

"Yes, there is," Lee said. "We can let the police handle it.

You know you haven't done anything wrong, as long as there's no law against stupidity. You don't have anything to fear."

"Tell that to—" The beep sounded in my ear. "Hi, Nolan," I spoke to the machine, "it's Kyle. Unfortunately, Lee and I are going to have to stay in Manhattan at least overnight. Something unexpected's come up, and I was wondering if you—"

"Hi there," Nolan's live voice suddenly broadcast over the phone. "Sorry, I was in the shower. Just heard the last ring as I turned off the water."

"Well, I'm glad you're there. I've got a problem." I then took the next several minutes explaining to Nolan the events of the day, judiciously editing out my public unveiling. Worse than Lee, Nolan would be absolutely unmerciful with his constant kidding. He'd never let me live it down.

"Is there anything you can do?" I ended with an appeal. As an ex-policeman who had conducted most of his law enforcement career in the Midwest, then in an unlikely move had finished it off with a two-year stint as a Manhattan homicide detective, Nolan had proved enormously helpful in several of my earlier encounters with the police.

"Well, I can certainly try, old buddy," he said. "What was the guy's name? Lockwood? By any chance, do you know his precinct?"

"I don't think he said," I answered truthfully, then I remembered that he had given Lee his card. "Lee," I yelled.

No answer. I yelled again. Still no response.

I lifted my hand from the mouthpiece. "I'm sorry, Nolan," I said. "I thought I could get the information from Lee, but she seems to have momentarily disappeared."

"Well, doesn't matter. I can track him down. Hey, you said you visited the scene of the crime. By any chance, do you remember the address?"

I did and dutifully recited it to him. "That's right on the precinct dividing line," he said by way of explanation, "but I'm pretty sure that the particular location you're describing would belong in the Sixth. The Mansard Building, you say? That name sounds familiar, and the address is definitely down in my old stomping grounds. Say, I know Captain Riley of the Sixth Precinct fairly well. I'll give him a call and see what I can find out. Couple other cops over there I can contact as well."

"Thanks," I said, and meant it.

"You really think you're a serious suspect?" I could hear the incredulity in his voice. "It's hard for me to believe."

"Nolan, right now I'm the only suspect."

"Don't start making your reservations for Sing Sing just quite yet," he commented, laughing with genuine amusement.

"That's easy for you to say."

"Stop worrying. I can't see anybody putting handcuffs on you, not for this murder anyway."

"I'm glad you're so positive."

"Look," Nolan explained patiently, "believe me, this guy Lockwood's just doing his job. But if it makes you feel any better, I'll be happy to talk to him too. He might even pay a little more attention to an old warhorse like me than to a young stallion like you."

"Come on, get off that 'old' kick. You're still on the light side of fifty—"

"Barely."

"Anyway, I think Lockwood's the stallion. He couldn't keep his eyes off Lee the whole time we were with him."

Nolan hooted. "Is that the green-eyed monster I hear snorting in the background?"

"I'm serious, Nolan. You should have seen the way the man looked at my wife. He was downright blatant about it, and believe me, I didn't like it one bit."

"She's seven months pregnant, for God's sake."

"That's what Lee said."

Nolan laughed. "Then she's being more sensible than you. I think you're overreacting because you find yourself behind the eight ball in this case. Just put it out of your mind. Let the police handle it."

"That's what Lee said, too."

"Then listen to her."

"Look, Nolan," I said, changing the subject, "I need to ask you a favor. Lockwood told us not to leave town, so Lee and I are stuck here for the immediate future. I don't know how long it'll be until we can get back up to Tipton. But I need—"

"Say no more. You want me to take care of your animals. Consider it done."

"I really appreciate it. If you could gather them up and take them back to your place—"

Again Nolan interrupted before I could finish my sentence. "Sure," he said, "no problem. I'll let 'em bed down with me." He paused. "Wait a minute. I just had a thought. Instead of uprooting them, why don't I just take my sleeping bag over to your house and camp out on your sofa?"

"That would be wonderful—if you're sure you don't mind?"

"Not a bit, it'll be my pleasure. Anyway, I can always pop back over here anytime I need to. After all, I'll just be next door."

"Great," I replied in grateful approval, then continued, "Just one thing—stay out of the La-Z-Boy, if you don't mind."

"Oh?"

"Yeah," I said, patiently explaining the reason, "if the ferret happened to be under it when—"

"I get the picture."

"If you need anything, just give us a call here." I gave him Lee's Manhattan telephone number, then, as an afterthought, the street address as well.

"Like I said, no sweat. I'll get things moving as soon as I get off the phone."

"You still have your key to my house, don't you?" I reminded him.

"Yep," Nolan said, "right here in my pocket. Now stop worrying. Everything's going to be fine."

That was a guarantee I'd have liked to believe.

CHAPTER **TEN**

*"The author
proves a master
at mixing
common, everyday ingredients
in order to concoct
the perfect mystery
soufflé."*

—Stokes Moran,
on Katherine Hall Page's *The Body in the Bog*

$\mathscr{I}$ had barely disconnected the call to Nolan when the telephone rang in my hand.

"Stokes Moran?" the caller asked.

"Yes," I answered automatically.

I heard a mocking laugh. "Isn't that interesting? And here I thought he was dead."

Lockwood.

I stiffened. "You're wrong. My Stokes Moran is very much alive."

"Oh really. I thought you told me you had killed him off."

"I've decided to bring him back to life."

He laughed again. "Isn't it too bad that we can't perform the same miracle on that poor stiff in the morgue?"

"Look, Lockwood," I said, my growing anger getting the better of me. "Did you have some purpose for calling, or do you just enjoy harassing innocent citizens?"

"I had a purpose for calling, all right. In fact, a couple of them."

He paused. When he didn't immediately continue, I demanded, "Well, are you going to enlighten me, or do I have to read your mind?" Easy, Kyle, don't antagonize the man, I inwardly cautioned.

"I was just trying to decide which to share with you first. The good news or the bad news?"

More games. I had grown tired of Lockwood's irritating manner six hours ago.

"Well?" he prompted.

"Oh, you're waiting for a response?" I said innocently. "I'm so sorry. I thought the question was rhetorical."

He ignored the gibe. "Since you don't seem to have a preference, I'll share the good news with you first."

Suddenly, Lockwood adopted a more professional tone. His bantering ended, and the conversation turned businesslike.

"The social security card turned out to be a forgery after all," he said. "The number belongs to a catfish farmer down in Mississippi. Still very much alive, by the way."

"Is that the good news?" I couldn't resist another dig.

"Part of it," he said, not taking the bait. "The fake card at least gives a little credibility to your theory that this was some kind of shakedown gone awry."

"Didn't I tell you? This proves—"

"This proves exactly nothing."

"What do you mean?"

"I mean," he drawled, "what the good computer giveth, it also taketh away."

I frowned, frustrated with this long-drawn-out exercise. "I'm afraid you're not making any sense."

"That Visa card turned out to be the real McCoy," he answered. "Or should I say the real Moran?"

"You're kidding!"

"Not at all." I could almost visualize the requisite shake

of his head. "The account is very much open. Authorized some nine months ago. With a fairly impressive credit line."

Nothing about this case made sense. I had been so certain that all those papers would prove false.

"And you're going to like this," Lockwood intruded on my thoughts.

From the almost gleeful tone in the detective's voice, I harbored no illusions that the information he was about to reveal wouldn't be to my liking at all.

"The address the company has for Stokes Moran is Seventeen River Bend, Tipton, Connecticut." He paused. "Sound familiar?"

Familiar? Of course it's familiar, you idiot. You know as well as I do that it's my home address. You wouldn't be dangling imaginary handcuffs in front of my eyes otherwise, now would you? But all I volunteered aloud was a cautionary "Yes."

While I may have succeeded somewhat in quelling the rising panic that threatened to engulf my rational mind, I was clearly rattled, and what's worse, Lockwood knew it. This latest bombshell provided the detective with an indisputable connection between me and the murdered man—the same address, impossible and inconceivable as it was. Ridiculously, in my mind's eye, I suddenly saw myself as the desperate Road Runner, with the wily adversary closing ground by the minute. Beep, beep. Boy, did I need a turbocharged escape.

But it wasn't quite as easy picturing Lockwood in the coyote part, playing the patented Acme brand of pursuit and invariably self-destructing at the last second. No, my mind just wouldn't accept that image, tempting though it might have been. Right now, Lockwood bore as little resemblance to a bumbling cartoon character as nightmare to daydream, but I was the one trapped in the nightmare. Lockwood was a constant and all too human menace, and his next words proved it.

"Mr. Malachi, can you offer any explanation how this man who you claim never to have known had in his possession a credit card assigned to Stokes Moran at your address?"

"No," I feebly admitted, "I can't explain it at all."

I hadn't expected his sudden silence. Maybe my lack of defense had caught him momentarily off guard. Pressing my nebulous advantage, I reminded him, "You earlier mentioned that the fake social security card was just part of the good news. Is there something more?"

Lockwood waited a second or two before he answered. "Yeah, though I really don't know what it means," he said finally.

"Maybe I can help," I prompted.

"I doubt it."

"Give it up, Lockwood. Tell me what it is!"

He laughed. "Simmer down. It's just that less than an hour after I fed the stiff's fingerprints into the NCIC, an assistant U.S. attorney was standing in my captain's office demanding information about the case."

"Is that unusual?"

"You better believe it. We normally don't get federal inquiries in person, especially not that fast."

Was now the time for me to tell Lockwood about Amy's "gummint" car? Didn't the unexpected intrusion into the case of a U.S. attorney add further support to the theory that a governmental agency was somehow involved in the murder? But something told me to keep quiet, at least for a little while longer.

"It makes me wonder," Lockwood speculated, not waiting for me to reply, "if maybe there's more here than meets the eye."

"That's what I've been telling you all along."

He laughed again. "So you have. But you will remain available, though, just in case?"

His last three words were a subtle reminder that, despite the encouraging possibility that someone else may indeed have been involved in the crime, Kyle Malachi nevertheless remained the name at the top of his current hit parade.

"And how's your pretty little wife?" Lockwood suddenly asked.

I had to grant him one thing, the man sure knew how to push my buttons.

"Taken," I said hotly, and hung up.

"Nolan been bending your ear all this time?"

I found Lee in the kitchen, meticulously dicing onions on a wooden butcher block. Arrayed around the countertop were an open jar of Grey Poupon, a bottle of sweet pickle relish, squeezable Cheez Whiz, a shaker of extra-hot chili powder, a tin of sardines, and a loaf of black rye bread.

"Not exactly," I said with a frown. "By the way, where were you? I called out, but you never answered."

"I was down the hall in the trash room."

I noted my wife's labor-intensive concentration. "What are you doing now?" I asked suspiciously.

"Making a sandwich." Lee pulled two slices of bread from the bag, dipped a knife into the mustard, and slathered thick globs of the pungent spread onto the rye. She then repeated the same actions with the relish.

"We just ate," I reminded her.

"That was three hours ago. Besides, you know Chinese food always makes me hungrier."

Lee slid the pile of minced onions off the cutting board and onto the mixture, added the Cheez Whiz, then liberally sprinkled chili powder over the bizarre combination, topped it off with several sardines, and finally slapped the two heavily laden pieces of bread together.

"What about the frozen yogurt?" I said absently.

"I finished that ages ago." I watched in disbelief as she raised the sandwich to her mouth.

"Any good?"

"Mmm," she said. "Here, have a bite."

I shook my head. "I don't think so."

"Go on." Lee pinched a corner off the sandwich and almost pushed the wedge between my lips. She then wolfed down the remainder of the sandwich in only three gulps.

"Now tell me what Nolan had to say," Lee said, licking the last vestiges of the sandwich from her fingers.

"Oh." I forced a swallow down my constricted throat. "Nolan said he'd be happy to stay with the animals."

"That's it? That's what you've been talking about for the last half hour?"

I watched in alarm as Lee reached for two more bread slices. "No, no, no," I said. She glanced crossly in my direction, arching her eyebrows in an unspoken question, daring me to voice any culinary criticism.

"It wasn't Nolan," I squeaked, clarifying my negatives. "Lockwood called." I then briefly summarized the gist of the detective's remarks, admitting a little guiltily that I had refrained from telling him about my encounter with Amy.

"Want a root beer?" she asked, pulling open the refrigerator door.

"No, thank you."

"So you still believe you're his prime suspect?"

"His only suspect."

My wife returned to the counter with two cans of Hires root beer, along with a container of sour cream and a jar of marshmallow paste.

"But he must have doubts, especially now that the U.S. attorney's gotten involved?"

I nodded, watching in horror as Lee constructed another sandwich, identical to the first except with the addition of large dollops of marshmallow and sour cream.

"Oh, this one's even better," she sighed with obvious pleasure. "Kyle, you've got to taste it." Lee extended the sandwich in my direction.

This time I clamped my jaws tight, shaking my head in vigorous refusal.

Lee laughed, chomping heartily, and in a feat worthy of Ripley finished off the last of the sandwich in record time, then followed it with a healthy swig of root beer.

"Why didn't you tell Lockwood about the bag lady's information?" Matching lids to jars and tops to bottles, Lee began tidying up the chaotic aftermath of her heroic sandwiches.

"I don't know. Something just told me not to."

She laughed. "Maybe it was nothing more than embarrassment."

I smiled. "You might have a point. If I couldn't even bring myself to tell Nolan, I'm sure not about to tell Lockwood."

With all the items now neatly returned to their rightful places in the kitchen, Lee swirled a wet dishcloth over the counter's surface, dislodging the last of the crumbs, propelling them anonymously to the floor.

"But is that the only reason?" My wife deposited the soiled rag into the sink and turned to face me.

"What do you mean?"

Lee laughed. "You're the mystery reader. You tell me."

I knew what Lee was implying. If this were a mystery novel, the amateur detective—and in this scenario I guess that would be me—would invariably withhold some vital piece of evidence that he might have stumbled across, thus allowing him as well as the reader to stay one step ahead of the doltish police and brilliantly outnose them to the finish line. As I saw it, there were just a couple of problems with that particular plot device. First, this was a real-life situation, with me not just the sleuth but also the suspect. And second, I had no earthly idea if Amy's information was in fact a crucial clue, or if it would merely lead nowhere. "Gummint" could quite easily turn out to be one of those infamous red herrings mystery writers always find so amusing and readers so infuriating. You just never knew.

"I'm sure Lockwood's keeping some things close to his vest too," I said in lieu of a direct answer to Lee's implication. "I think he's only telling what he wants us to know, and no more."

"You're awfully cynical about Lockwood."

"You'd be cynical too if you were the one he was after." I stopped, suddenly recognizing the double meaning to my words. "Forget I said that."

Lee laughed. "Oh, you." She punched me affectionately on the shoulder. "I keep reminding you I'm seven months pregnant."

I leaned my head toward her face and planted a kiss on her forehead. "And I keep reminding you how attractive you are."

She reached her arms around my neck and nibbled my left ear with her lips. "Thank you."

A few minutes later, I opened the freezer. "Where's my chocolate swirl with almond chips?"

Lee looked chagrined. "I'm afraid I ate your yogurt along with mine."

"You're worse than the Salvation Army. No food's safe around you."

"What else do you expect from an expectant mother?"

I reached for a jar of olives and had barely unscrewed the top when Lee's hand suddenly shot out and snagged the bottle from my grip.

"Mmm." She eagerly tipped the jar back against her lips, filling her mouth with the pitted green goodies and lapping up the vinegary brine as well. "Sorry," she mumbled, still in mid-chew, "but as you said, no food's safe around me."

I felt no regret over the lost olives. Lee's action had reminded me of Amy—Amy the voracious scavenger, the lightning-quick retriever, the greedy pack rat. And then through the lens of my internal camera I panned over to the nearby grocery cart, roped so possessively to her and filled to overflowing, presumably containing all her worldly possessions—society's discarded trash, the bag lady's keenly guarded treasure.

Amy—the human vacuum cleaner.

CHAPTER **ELEVEN**

"When Toby stashes Bette Davis
away in a two-bit hotel,
what reader
can resist anticipating
her signature pronouncement,
'What a dump!'"

—Stokes Moran,
on Stuart M. Kaminsky's *The Devil Met a Lady*

"Are you crazy?" I can't say Lee's reaction was all that surprising.

"At this time of night?"

Or unexpected.

"In that part of town?"

Or without merit.

"You've lost your senses."

Or unreasonable.

I patiently offered no interruptions. "If you think it's that all-fired important for you to go see that awful bag lady again, then I don't understand why you can't at least wait until tomorrow morning. In the daylight. Any sane person would."

Lee waddled over to the sofa and collapsed against its overstuffed cushions. "I doubt that old woman'll be going anywhere in the meantime, and how do you know she'll even be in the same place? Besides, my feet hurt." For verification, she tried to rub her right ankle, but her reach extended only a little bit below the knee.

"I didn't say you had to go too."

"Not go? Do you think I'm about to let you traipse off down there alone? Not on your life." She pushed herself up from her seat. "Anyway, what kind of wife would I be? You could get yourself killed."

"It's not exactly skid row," I reminded her. "I should be quite safe."

"Need I remind you," Lee commented sarcastically as she regained her feet, "that in some parts of town, there's no such thing as safe."

Lee walked toward the door.

"Well?" she asked, opening the closet and retrieving her coat. "What's keeping you?"

I shook my head in admiring amazement, then quickly scampered after her.

Lee drove, although it would probably have been easier to hop in a cab.

She picked a route that landed us smack in the middle of Broadway just at peak show time, where traffic moved more slowly than a hog-tied elephant. From our current vantage point at the Fiftieth Street crossing, I glimpsed an unbroken yellow sea of taxicabs that ebbed and flowed all the way to the Times Square delta. Clearly, at this moment, my wife was in no mood for criticism of her choice of route, constructive or otherwise.

It didn't take a mind reader to recognize my wife's silent fury or that it was directed not so much at the snarled traffic as at me. *Why do you always have to be so pigheaded?* I could almost hear her say. *Why can't you let the police handle it? Why are you so determined to solve this case yourself?* And finally: *Why did you get us into this mess in the first place?*

For that last question, I had no defensible answer. My rash decision to kill off Stokes Moran—had it only been twenty-eight hours ago?—had obviously been the key that opened this particular Pandora's box. And for that, I had no one but myself to blame. If, as it looked now, my actions eventually landed me in a courtroom, I could imagine my plea. *Your Honor,* I would attest, *it's simply a case of temporary insanity,* a claim in which my wife would no doubt heartily concur. Except she might dispute the temporary nature of my condition and toss in gross stupidity just for good measure.

Admittedly, Lee didn't view the situation in quite the life-and-death extremes that I did. She saw Lockwood more as an ally while I on the other hand pictured him in purely adversarial terms—hunter versus quarry, executioner versus martyr, Roman versus Christian, with all thumbs down, and me thrown to the hungry lions.

Somehow I had to convince Lee that this was more than a joke gone bad, that I was indeed in a serious jam. A man lay dead, and as far as the police were concerned, I was the prime—sole—suspect. Why didn't Lee understand that I just couldn't rely blithely on Lockwood and Pride to clear my name? I had to do it myself. And for me to succeed, I had to have Lee in my corner. But first I had to get us back on speaking terms.

After another ten minutes of uneasy silence between us, I decided to risk a conversational diversion.

"How are you coming with baby names?"

"What?"

"The baby will be here in about two months," I reminded her. "Don't you think it's about time we discussed some names?"

"You were the one who vetoed the amniocentesis, remember? Or do I need to remind you what you said?"

I didn't need reminding, but Lee didn't pause for my

response. "You said you didn't want to know the outcome of a good mystery novel until the author revealed it. Just like everything else in your life, you equate the birth of our child with a damn mystery story."

"I—"

"Yes, you do. Don't try to deny it." Lee turned her head away from me, but I could see the tears forming in the corners of her eyes. "And I just bet you want to name the baby after some damn mystery writer."

I reached for her shoulder, but she shrugged my hand away. "I'm right, aren't I? So, what have you come up with? Something like Raymond Chandler Malachi, I bet? Or Ellery Queen Malachi? No, let me guess—Agatha Christie Malachi? That's it, isn't it?" In the backwash from the streetlights, I could see the tears glistening on her cheeks. "Well?"

"To be honest," I said as sheepishly as I could manage, "I was thinking more on the order of Annie Laurance Malachi."

Lee was momentarily silenced, then she abruptly burst into laughter. "You asshole," she said, "you've got me blubbering like an idiot."

"That's better than hating me." I leaned over and brushed my lips against her ear.

"I don't hate you," she said, turning her face toward mine. "But sometimes you just make me so mad."

"I'm terrible," I whispered as I kissed the corners of her eyes and followed the tear tracks down her cheeks.

"Yes, you are," she murmured, but I found a wide grin on her mouth by the time mine reached hers. Then later, she added hoarsely, "You'll get us arrested."

"I hope you have cash this time," Lee warned fifteen minutes later as she braked for the signal at the corner of Broadway and Eleventh.

"I brought something even better," I answered, proudly

patting the pint of Jim Beam that now rested securely inside my jacket's breast pocket. Snatching it had been a last-minute inspiration on my part as we had left the apartment.

"I can just imagine what it is. What am I going to do the next time I get thirsty?"

"Try water."

Since neither Lee nor I usually drank anything stronger than club soda, I knew the whiskey had most likely been pre-sented to Lee by one of her grateful former clients, possibly as a Christmas gift she was too polite to refuse and too parsi-monious to throw away. Luckily for me.

Still without my money clip—why hadn't I remembered to ask Lockwood for its return?—I harbored no desire for a repeat of this afternoon's embarrassing command performance. I hoped Amy preferred Jim Beam in the bottle to Kyle Malachi in the flesh.

"Just pull in next to the curb," I suggested as Lee made a left turn, bumping across the unevenly repaired potholes.

Ten yards later, Lee braked to a stop. Unlike earlier in the day, no vehicles lined either side of the narrow street, and the corner lamplight cast little illumination this far into the block. The entrance of the building was obscured in shadows, but I could discern a dark shape lying unmoving against the steps. Amy? I certainly hoped so.

"Well, here goes," I announced to Lee, mustering a false bravado. As I opened the passenger door and stepped out onto the pavement, I experienced an involuntary chilling shudder down the back of my neck. True, the outside tem-perature had dropped considerably since the afternoon, but somehow I didn't think that was quite the explanation for my uncontrollable shiver. Why did images from Stephen King have to pop into my mind at just this second? Lee had been right. Even though we were only a few dozen yards away from the well-lighted activity of Broadway and Eleventh, this loca-tion was definitely not a place I'd normally choose to visit in the dark of night, and I was intensely appreciative of my wife's presence. But even with Lee's comforting proximity, I was suddenly and inexplicably spooked.

"Lock the doors," I called to Lee as I approached her side of the Land Rover. "And whatever you do, don't get out of the car."

"Why, Kyle? What's wrong?"

"Just do as I say." My fear must have communicated itself to her because without further protest I heard the locks snap in place. "And keep the windows rolled up."

I think it was the absolute absence of sound that had alarmed me. This was Manhattan, after all, and, with the possible exception of the depths of Central Park, there was no place in this city that should ever be this quiet, this eerily still at any hour of the day or night. There should have been some movement, some noise. A busy thoroughfare was only half a block or so away. Yet it was as if a soundproof wall had descended around me or somehow I had wandered into a silent catacomb. I found myself walking on tiptoes toward the recumbent form.

"Amy?"

No response. She lay face down against the cold stone, her ragged clothes covering her featureless shape. I suppose she could have been sleeping off a bender, but I had my doubts. I'd always heard that street people wake in an instant, since their very lives might depend on their remaining ever vigilant. Amy had not stirred at either my approach or the call of her name. Kneeling down beside her body, I reached my hand out to touch her.

"Amy?" I said again, grabbing her right shoulder to shake her awake.

Abruptly she rolled into me, knocking me off balance. Caught unprepared, I couldn't brace myself in time, and I sprawled backward, sitting down hard against the cement, the breath momentarily robbed from my lungs. In the same motion Amy fell into my arms, her head coming to rest against my chest, her eyes open, her lips parted, an obscene mockery of seduction.

She was dead. I knew it before I searched for a pulse, before I felt the coolness of her skin, before I glimpsed the blood on the front of her shirt. Somehow I had known it even before I had touched the body. Death had stamped its mark on this place.

Behind me, I heard the door of the Land Rover creak open. "Kyle?" Lee called.

"Get back in the car!"

"But—"

"Now!"

The car door slammed in compliance. I turned my attention once again to the dead body still nestling against me. Curled around Amy's waist, I spotted the familiar frayed rope, but now it hung loose, the end neatly severed, connected to nothing. I quickly scanned the immediate vicinity. Where was the shopping cart? Had Amy been killed for what it contained? Had she chosen to die rather than surrender her few worldly goods to a thief? What prize could she possibly have possessed that was worth the value of a human life?

Or was there more to this killing than just a simple mugging? Was it somehow—?

I suddenly realized the implication. The police could connect me to two murders in as many days. Coincidence? They'd never buy it. I scrambled to my feet. I had to get out of here now. And fast.

As I disentangled myself from Amy's body, her right arm—pinned against me for the last few minutes—fell limp atop the steps, and I noticed that she held something clutched tightly in her right hand. It was one of my argyle socks! Without thinking, I reached down and ripped it from her grip. Desperately, I looked around for anything else that might identify my presence at the scene.

Nothing. As best I could determine, Amy wasn't wearing any of the items—shirt, pants, shoes—she'd recently extorted from me. Nor were they anywhere else in plain sight. The killer must have taken them along with Amy's other belongings.

But just to make certain, I bent down beside her and hurriedly rifled through the numerous layers of clothing she wore, checking all the folds and pockets. Satisfied that no telltale items remained that could conceivably link me to the dead woman, I once again stood up.

Fingerprints? The idea made me shudder with fright. What had I touched? Could the police lift fingerprints from cloth or skin? I didn't think so, but then I couldn't be sure. I was just about to use the sock to wipe away any possible prints when I realized how cold and sticky it felt in my hand.

That's when I opened my palm and saw the blood.

CHAPTER **TWELVE**

"He's found standing
over the dead woman's body,
her blood
on his hands.
As the evidence mounts against him,
why does he still refuse to
talk?"

—Stokes Moran,
on Sophie Dunbar's *Behind Eclaire's Doors*

" *K*yle, you've got to call the police."

"I can't."

Hardly a minute had elapsed since the moment I had jerked open the passenger door and shouted, "Drive!"

Lee gunned the motor, made a U-turn in the middle of the street, barely braked at the corner to check for oncoming traffic, and then fishtailed out into the intersection.

"You don't have any other choice," she said, straightening out the wild turn and heading back north. "Kyle, you can't run away from this."

"Look." I turned to face my wife, grateful that we had survived her Evel Knievel stunt driving. "It's too late. I'm already guilty of leaving the scene of a crime, disturbing the body, removing evidence, and who knows what else. I've got to come up with some sort of explanation before I tell the cops anything."

"Why can't you just tell them the truth?" Lee accelerated through a yellow light.

I frowned. "Are you crazy? Who'd believe me? With Lockwood already breathing down my neck for one murder, what do you think he'll do when he catches me in another?"

"I—"

"I'll tell you what he'll do," I said. "He'll lock me up and throw away the key, that's what he'll do."

"You can't be sure—"

I laughed. "Lee, don't kid yourself. Lockwood is not our friend. He'll arrest me in a heartbeat."

"You don't know that."

"Yes, I do. And with me behind bars, he'll be able to close the books on two murders, which will allow the real killer to get clean away."

Lee frowned, emphatically shaking her head. "I don't like it."

"Neither do I," I answered. "But I've got to do this my way."

"Why?" Lee abruptly veered the Land Rover into the left lane, zooming past a slow-moving city bus. "Don't you think it's just possible you might be wrong about all this?" she said.

I shook my head. "No, I don't. As I see it, the only chance I've got to clear my name is for me to solve these murders myself. And, believe me, that's not something I can accomplish from inside a jail cell."

"Then what are you going to do?" she demanded as she slammed on the horn for an out-of-state driver who had the temerity to obey the legal limit.

"As soon as we get back to the apartment," I said, my decision already made, "I'm going to call Nolan."

"And you're sure no one saw you?" he asked.

This time I had told Nolan everything, even the omissions

from my first little adventure with Amy. When he didn't interrupt with his usual wisecracking asides, I knew I was in trouble. Normally Nolan's a cross between David Letterman and Mister Rogers, but tonight I got Inspector Maigret instead.

"Is it as bad as I think it is?" I asked after I'd ended my recitation of the pertinent events.

"Well, it's not good," he finally admitted after a ten-second silence. "I can understand why you didn't want to call the police, but unfortunately Lockwood doesn't know you as well as I do."

"Lucky me," I muttered.

"Look at it from his point of view," Nolan continued, studiously ignoring my offhand comment. "Two murders on two successive nights at the same location. And what's the one common link?" He paused for dramatic effect, then delivered the payoff. "You."

"But right now, Lockwood doesn't even know I was there," I argued. "And who says he ever has to?"

"He'll find out," Nolan predicted.

"How can you be so sure? I told you nobody saw me."

"One thing I learned from all my years in police work," he pontificated, "somebody always sees something. And sooner or later, all the secrets come out. Let's just hope your particular secret stays hidden just a little bit longer than the real killer. Cops are always a lot more understanding once the case is solved."

"Then let's solve it," I suggested.

"Look," he said sternly, "the best thing for you to do right now is just sit tight, keep your mouth shut, and let me see what I can find out."

"You want me to do nothing?" I asked incredulously. "You want me just to sit here and wait for Lockwood to come and get me?"

"That's right. There's nothing else you can do. You're not the cop on the beat. You have no leads to follow, no clues to figure out, no suspects to interview. The situation's bad enough as it is. I don't want you making it even worse."

"I don't see how that's possible," I said morosely.

"Then take my advice and leave it alone."

I didn't give him a direct answer. Instead, I asked about the animals.

"Bootsie and Wee are fine," he said. "They've both been on their best behavior, two little angels, not causing any problems at all. Which is why I know they miss you. They're not acting normal." He laughed.

I joined in the laughter. "It couldn't be anywhere near as much as I miss them. Life's just not the same without them underfoot."

"You got that right."

We talked another couple of minutes, then said our goodbyes. As I disconnected the call, I was still remembering Nolan's stern admonitions—"sit tight" and "leave it alone."

He obviously didn't know me as well as he thought.

"Why are you still wearing your jacket?" Lee asked, walking into the living room from the kitchen, an open jar of crunchy peanut butter in one hand, an oversized spoon in the other.

"I guess I was in such a hurry to talk to Nolan I just forgot I had it on," I answered, shrugging the coat off my shoulders. As I folded the abandoned garment over the sofa, something clanged against the wooden backboard.

"Don't leave it there," Lee grumbled, the spoon halfway to her mouth. "Hang it in the closet."

I slipped my hand into the jacket's inside pocket and retrieved the pint of whiskey I'd intended to barter to Amy. Now she'd never have the pleasure of making its acquaintance.

As I returned the Jim Beam to its original position on the top shelf of the credenza near the front door, I remembered something else I'd stashed inside the jacket. I reached into the right outside pocket and pulled out the blood-soaked sock.

I looked down at the single argyle sock, somehow appearing utterly ridiculous without its mate. I held in my hand evidence the police would undoubtedly associate with my guilt. After all, the victim had been clutching it when she died.

What should I do with it? Destroy it? Keep it? Clean it and wash away the blood and perhaps other potential evidence as well? Then stow it away neatly in my sock drawer with all the other argyle orphans? Or would that get me in too much trouble? Oh well, I suppose I had already committed a crime by removing the sock in the first place, so I guess it didn't much matter what I did with it now. My wife could tell you firsthand that there's no such thing as being a little bit pregnant. She'd say flat out, "Either you are or you aren't." Same thing with the law. There were no half measures. Either you played by the rules or you didn't.

And, believe me, thus far I hadn't. But I felt I had justifiable cause. But just how persuasive would my reasons sound to a judge?

Your Honor, I could hear myself say, the way I rationalized it, the deed had been done. Tampering was tampering, and I'd already crossed that threshold. If the police had discovered that I'd removed the sock from the scene of the crime in the first place, would it have then mattered what I did with it afterward?

Whether my imaginary judge would agree with me or not, I made my decision and headed for the utility room and Lee's washer-dryer combination. Once there, I reached for the detergent and opened the lid of the washing machine. Then, out of long habit, I turned the sock inside out, as my mother had always taught me. That's when the matchbook fell to the floor.

With growing excitement, I bent down and picked it up.

On the front, the name Tootsie's was stenciled in pink script against a black background, fluffy feather boas encircling the single word. On the back, in small white-on-black type, appeared a corresponding address and telephone number.

From long practice and stifling a sudden cigarette craving, I flipped open the matchbook. Inside the front cover, someone had penciled the word TIPTON in bold block letters. Then, behind the rows of matches, I spotted a jagged piece of paper. I carefully fished it out with my fingertips. It was a picture of a man I'd briefly glimpsed only once before. But I would never forget that face or the circumstances under which I'd seen it.

Earlier today.

In three pictures.

Lying on a cold table.

Covered by a single white sheet.

In the morgue.

Gingerly, I now held between my thumb and forefinger a torn picture of the man Lockwood persisted in calling Stokes Moran.

I had been right! Amy had indeed scavenged something valuable after all. Even without the Jim Beam, she had come through like a trouper. Good old Amy! I suddenly felt like a death-row inmate who's just received a last-minute reprieve from the governor. I now had new hope, new energy, new life.

Even better, I now had a clue.

CHAPTER **THIRTEEN**

*"The detective
comes to the ultimate realization
that only in understanding
the true identity of the victim
will there ever be a chance
of finally unmasking
the killer."*

—Stokes Moran,
on Natasha Cooper's *Bloody Roses*

"*Y*ou can't be serious," Lee objected, propped up in bed with the latest Nevada Barr mystery novel lying companionably across her lap and a cup of hot cocoa and an open box of Smores sitting within easy arm's reach on the nearby nightstand. "It's almost midnight, and we've put in a very long day already."

"I don't expect you to go."

"Well, I'm certainly glad to hear that."

"But I need more cash," I admitted, carefully avoiding any outright criticism of my frugal wife. "I'll probably need more than the fifty you got from the automatic teller machine. Cab fare, cover charges, who knows what I'll run into down there." I laughed nervously. "And please remind me tomorrow to get my money clip back from Lockwood."

"Why do you have to take a cab? Why not just drive the Land Rover?" she suggested.

I shook my head. "I hate parking, and, unlike you, I'm not willing to push my luck by parking in tow-away zones."

"How do you know the place'll even be open?"

"I called. The woman who finally answered the phone said they didn't close till five A.M."

"What's the name of this place again?"

"Tootsie's."

"Never heard of it."

"What difference does that make?" I demanded, perhaps a bit too impatiently.

She frowned. "I just don't like the idea of my husband going off alone in the middle of the night to some strange place we've never heard of. Without me," she added.

"I'll be fine."

"But why the hurry? I don't see why this can't wait until tomorrow."

"Because I can't wait until tomorrow. I want to follow up on this now. This is the first lead I've had, and as wired as I am, I wouldn't be able to sleep anyway. So I might as well do it now."

My wife changed tactics. "You know I don't carry cash."

"Yes, I know. But I also know you keep some on hand for taxicabs, pizza deliveries, tips, and so forth. So come clean, where is it?"

Lee sighed. "It's over there in the top drawer of my dresser." She waved her arm in the general direction. "But don't take it all."

Underneath two paperback thrillers and a floral scarf, I found two twenties and a ten nestling next to assorted keys, earrings, pens and pins, and other odds and ends. "I'm borrowing thirty dollars—a twenty and a ten. Eighty bucks should just about cover any eventuality." I added the two bills to my fifty, turned them all in the same direction, folded them neatly together, and tucked them securely in my right pants pocket.

"Be careful," Lee warned.

As I headed out the door, maybe I only imagined her parting words.

"Fat chance."

Felipe, the night-shift doorman, insisted on flagging the taxi for me. Claiming poverty, I offered him my thanks and promised a tip the next time. He nodded as if not totally convinced of my trustworthiness.

Nighttime is Manhattan's shining moment, and I've always felt that the best way to appreciate the city's grandeur and spectacle is from the backseat of a taxicab. That way, you force an anonymous ferrier to contend with the worries and hassles of traffic while you're safely isolated from the urban jungle. You can just sit back and absorb the majestic sights and sounds of the world's most exciting metropolis without any of the incumbent worry. All in all, it's not a bad way to take a delicious bite out of the Big Apple.

But tonight I was no mere tourist. Instead I was Rambo on a mission, Columbo on a case, Sherlock on a scent. I could feel the adrenaline pulsing through my body, validating the excitement of the chase.

As the taxi driver hurtled me south on Columbus, I reflected on the rush of events of the past thirty-two hours. Thirty-two hours? It didn't seem possible. Hard to believe that it had only been yesterday afternoon that I had inadvertently set all this chaos in motion. Less than a short day and a half and yet the course of my life seemed inalterably changed. And just as dramatically, just as suddenly, all it took was one little matchbook, one slim clue, and I no longer felt quite so desperate and defeated. I now had a chance to once again assert control over my own life, I had a direction. I rolled down the back window and reveled in the shock of the cold night air. Was it a euphoria such as this that energized Lew Archer and Kinsey Millhone—coming from nothing more than a simple break in a particularly difficult case? A clue that in truth might lead absolutely nowhere?

But it was leading me somewhere—the West Side neighborhood of Chelsea. Not exactly my choice as a worldly nirvana, but right now I wouldn't trade it for the Trump Tower. Chelsea lacked some of the eccentricity of its next-door neighbor, Greenwich Village, but this district of Manhattan nevertheless had its own distinctive style and flavor. The residents took earthly delight in Chelsea's quaint charm and oddball characters. What I might encounter at Tootsie's was anyone's guess.

The cabbie eventually turned onto Ninth Avenue and headed south toward Twenty-third. Five minutes later, after one further turn, he braked in front of a nondescript row of double-story structures.

"Is this it?" I asked, dubiously looking out the window at the unmarked buildings.

The driver confirmed the address in his Pakistani-accented English.

"Okay, if you say so." Still harboring my doubts, I handed him the ten-dollar bill and stepped out onto the sidewalk. He pulled away from the curb even as I slammed the door behind me.

Now what? The street sported no pedestrians, no lights shone in any of the buildings, and I couldn't find any identifying numbers on any of the doorways. For lack of anything better to do, I started walking. Ten paces later, I noticed a narrow space, barely wide enough for a person to squeeze through, between two of the buildings.

Taking what courage I had left, I edged through the opening. A barely legible sign over a solid-steel door told me I had arrived at Tootsie's. I pushed against the door and entered a world of impenetrable blackness. I stood unmoving for at least a minute before my eyes developed enough night vision to allow me to identify a flight of stairs rising to my right. I started up.

I heard the music before I saw the door, a steel twin to the one below. The instant I breached its closure, reverberating cacophonous sound blasted over me. I crossed the threshold.

A New York Giants reject sat enclosed in a cubicle to my left. He spoke to me through a speaker box midway up the glass partition.

"Upstairs or down?" he asked.

"What?" I shouted over the unrelenting din.

"Upstairs or down?"

"What's the difference?"

"Twenty bucks."

I wondered if anyone appreciated his deadpan delivery. Even him.

"You don't understand—" I started to say.

He grimaced, as if he was accustomed to this perplexed confusion. "Upstairs is for lookin', down is for mixin'."

Whatever that meant.

I reached in my pocket and pulled out the matchbook. Carefully I pressed the scrap of photograph against the glass.

"Can you tell me anything about this?"

"See Rhonda," he answered without inflection. "She's the one takes the pictures."

"Where can I find her?"

"Downstairs."

"I just came from downstairs."

"Through there." He motioned with his head to a doorway on my right.

"How will I know Rhonda?"

"She's the one with the camera." This guy was missing out on a great career opportunity. He should have been headlining at a comedy club.

I walked over to the door and tried the knob. It was locked in place. Why was I not surprised? I turned back to the man.

"Twenty bucks?" I asked.

"Twenty bucks."

The bottom of this stairway opened onto a dance floor. Several couples crowded into the narrow space, pulsating to the jungle beat. A glittering mirrored ball twirled and twinkled just inches above their heads. Half a dozen tables skirted the perimeter, the tops covered with red checkerboard tablecloths while glass-encased flickering candles provided ghostly illumination. All the seats around the tables appeared to be taken. I wondered if the people in the chairs periodically exchanged places with the dancers on the floor. Otherwise what happened to the overflow?

I edged closer to the action. A flashbulb unexpectedly went off in my face.

"Rhonda?"

"Do I know you?" she asked.

"Is there someplace we can talk away from this noise?"

She frowned for a moment, then nodded compliance. "Twenty bucks."

Is everything in this hellhole twenty bucks? I lamented. Damn Lee and her "don't take it all." I should have swiped more of her money. I was already down thirty bucks, and I had to save at least ten for the cab fare home. But I was desperate, so I coughed up the twenty.

"I want to ask you about this man." I held the photograph toward her. "Do you know him?"

She squinted at the jagged scrap of paper I cupped between my fingers. A look of sudden recognition crossed her face.

"Follow me," she said abruptly.

Rhonda threaded her way among the gyrating dancers, with me hard on her heels. She led a twisted path to a beaded doorway on the other side of the dance floor. I followed her through the opening.

We entered a long hallway to our left, with several closed doors dotting either side. Rhonda walked halfway down the corridor, opened a door on the right, and ushered me in. She closed the door behind us.

The room was small, no more than ten feet square, the carpet scuffed and dirty. The walls, absent any decoration, were a dingy gray, and only a single threadbare sofa passed as furniture. An uncovered hundred-watt bulb in the middle of the ceiling emitted a harsh unflattering light. It was a depressing room, but I have to admit that the enveloping silence was as welcome to my abused eardrums as balm to parched lips.

"Thank you," I acknowledged gratefully. "This is so much better."

She laughed. "I misunderstood you at first. I'm sorry. I thought you meant something else besides just talk."

"I don't understand."

"I don't normally bring trade back here. I make my money strictly off the tourist shots. But you're a real looker, so I decided what the hell."

"You've lost me."

She laughed again. "Forget it. You wanted to know something about the john in that picture?"

A big-boned woman, Rhonda stood at eye level with me. Her long, straight blond hair, hanging almost to the waist of her skintight black sequined dress, further accentuated her height. But it was her crystal blue eyes that truly commanded attention. I decided had she gone a little bit easier on that heavy makeup, she'd have been a real looker too.

"Yeah," I said. "Anything you can tell me."

"He almost broke my camera, I can tell you that. Ripped it right out of my hands. Snapped a couple of my nails off." She looked down at her expertly manicured hands. "Then he snatched the print when it came out, waited for it to develop, and tore his face out of it."

"Why did he do that?"

"He obviously objected to having his picture taken. I've had guys object before, but never quite so violently."

"When was this?"

"Couple of nights ago, I think. Yeah, Wednesday it was."

"About what time?"

"One, two A.M. Something around that."

"Did you get his name?"

"Not bloody likely." She smiled. "Names don't matter a whole lot in a place like this."

"Did he say anything?"

"Called me a bitch, for one thing. I don't remember if he actually said anything else. Then he shoved the damaged print back in my hands."

As cooperative as Rhonda was proving, her information just wasn't getting me any closer to solving the man's identity. I was getting frustrated. And a little bit worried.

"How long was he here?"

"Couple of hours, I guess. I didn't pay that close attention."

"Did he talk to anyone else?"

She closed her eyes in concentration. "I think he and some other guy came back here for a while."

"Came back here? For what?"

She laughed. "You'd have to ask Trixie about that," she said mysteriously.

"Trixie? Who's Trixie?"

"She's one of the regulars."

"But what's she got to do with this man?"

"Didn't I tell you? Trixie was his date for the evening."

While Rhonda went back out front to see if she could locate Trixie, I realized I'd learned more about the bogus Stokes Moran than I'd initially thought. Here was a man who, for whatever reason, reacted violently to having his picture taken. Why? His behavior would certainly be consistent with my theory that he was in some way connected to the mob, perhaps even a hired killer. In such an event, it would be reasonable for the man to ferociously guard his identity.

Was I then a target of the Mafia? If that were the case, what was the purpose of the elaborate impersonation of Stokes Moran? Extortion would seem to be the answer to the latter question, but it completely contradicted the notion of a hit man. After all, why kill the goose you were hoping to fleece?

The sudden opening of the door delayed further reflection.

"I'm Trixie," she said, her voice reminding me of the throaty Lauren Bacall, except this one had a pronounced Southern drawl. "Rhonda told me that you wanted to talk to me."

The woman standing in the doorway was as much a counterpoint to Rhonda as two opposites can be. Petite, almost fragile, Trixie shimmered in a floor-length gown of white satin, split to the thigh at the sides, her stiletto heels possibly raising her to a height of five feet five. Lustrous raven hair framed an oval face, fine-boned, her skin nearly translucent. She looked as sculpted and as ephemeral as a porcelain figurine.

"Yes," I said quickly, covering my momentary lapse.

"Fifty bucks."

Here we go again, except this one was even more expensive. "I just want to ask you a couple of questions."

"Look, buster, I don't care what you want. I don't do nothin' 'less you cough up some dough."

"I've only got thirty left," I said, pulling the last bills out of my pocket. I'd just have to hope Lee's doorman would cover the cab fare when I got home. At least until I could get back downstairs and repay him.

"Oh, all right." She grabbed the twenty and the ten and stuffed it underneath her shoulder strap. She sat down on the sofa and kicked off her shoes. "Got a cigarette?"

"I'm sorry," I said, more than a little regretfully. "I gave up the habit."

"Too bad." She slipped her right hand through the slit in her dress. I heard something rip, then she pulled a crumpled pack of Virginia Slims from beneath the cloth. "Have to keep 'em taped to the inside of my leg," she explained. "Else they mess up the lines." She tamped the pack against her left palm, dislodging first an ultra-thin Bic lighter, followed by a rumpled cigarette that she straightened out before lighting. She then leaned against the back of the sofa, crossed her shapely legs, and took the first drag. My mouth watered in frustrated envy.

"Okay, shoot," she said.

I recovered quickly enough to proffer her the jagged photo. "Rhonda told me you know this man."

She laughed, a deep-throated guttural guffaw. "Yeah, I know him, if you can call it that," she confirmed, then appended, "Lousy tipper."

"What can you tell me about him? Do you know his name? Where he lives? What he does? Anything?"

"Easy, fella," she said. "Don't get in such a hurry. Here. Sit down." She patted the space on the sofa next to her. "You're givin' me a headache cranin' my neck up to look at you."

I sat. "Well?"

"Called himself Zack. Had just gotten in from . . . Detroit, I think it was." She frowned in concentration. "Yeah, Detroit. That was it, I'm pretty sure."

I waited for Trixie to continue, but when she didn't, I asked, "What else?"

She shrugged. "I don't know. He was just a john lookin' for a jill."

"What do you mean?"

"Some of the guys who come into the club just want to drink, dance, hold a pretty girl in their arms for a few hours. Others want something more."

"And he was one of those?"

"Yeah," she answered. "Him and his friend."

"The guy Rhonda told me about? The guy that your friend Zack supposedly met here?"

She nodded in agreement. "Yeah, seemed like a pre-arranged meet to me."

"What can you tell me about him? About this other guy?"

"Well, for one thing, he was local. Seen him in here two, maybe three times before. Pretty certain he's the one that picked the meetin' place."

"Then the two men didn't know each other before that night?"

"That's the impression I got."

"What did they talk about?"

"Just stuff. Nothin' in particular."

"That can't be."

"Mister, I was with Zack the whole time he was here." Then Trixie gave a vocal underline to her next sentence: "Before the other dude arrived, every minute the other dude was here, and even after the other dude left." She dropped the spent cigarette on the floor and ground it into the carpet with her heel. "Believe me, I didn't hear nothin' interestin'."

"But there must have been some exchange of information. Otherwise why have the meeting?"

"There was one thing."

"What?"

"He wrote somethin' down in one of our matchbooks, then handed it over to Zack. That was right before we all three came back here."

"What was this other guy's name?"

"Joe, leastways that's what he said." Trixie shot me a conspiratorial wink. "Pretty original, huh?"

"You mean you didn't believe him?"

She laughed that sexy throaty laugh again. "You think the Man's gonna give out with his real name?"

"The Man?" I asked. "You mean he was a cop?"

"Cop. Fed. Immigration. Somethin' like that. I can't

exactly tell you his rank and serial number. To me a Suit is a Suit. I can pick one out in Times Square at Halloween, and I can damn sure spot one even when he's in drag."

Drag? "You mean he came here dressed like a woman?"

Trixie's eyes opened wide, then she shook her head and smiled. "Which planet are you from?"

"What do you mean?"

"You're cute but you sure are dense. Here, I've got an idea. Why don't we do it this way instead." Trixie uncrossed her legs, slipped her hand through the slit, and adjusted something under her dress. She withdrew her hand and reached for mine. Then she gently guided my hand through the slit, across her warm thigh, and up into her crotch.

I jerked back my hand as if it had been scalded and abruptly stood up.

"Don't be so shocked, sweetie," she said. "What kind of place did you think Tootsie's was, anyway?"

"Y-y-you're a man!" I stammered.

"Congratulations." She laughed. "The light finally dawns."

"And you're a trans—" In my agitation, I couldn't grasp the word.

"Transvestite. It ain't so hard to say."

"But you look so real."

This time she laughed even more raucously. "I am real, honey."

"That's not what I meant."

She nodded. "I know what you meant. Your sum-total experience has probably only been in watchin' Robin Williams still recognizable in *Mrs. Doubtfire,* or Dustin Hoffman in *Tootsie*—from which this place obviously took its name. Or maybe you'd rather believe we're all as obvious as the TV prostitutes you see each week on the tabloids. It's easier for you to smugly think that's the way it is, that you can always tell when it's a man. Well, I'm a professional, and believe me, it's only the amateurs you can spot." She leaned over, reached under the sofa for her heels, and slipped the spiked shoes back on her feet.

"And Rhonda?"

"Yep."

I suddenly felt dizzy. "So that means this cop Joe's a transvestite too?"

Trixie stood up. "No," she said simply.

"No?"

"No. Joe's a cross-dresser."

I frowned in confusion. "I thought that was the same thing."

"It's not." Then she explained patiently, as if by rote, "A cross-dresser is a man who just likes to wear women's clothes, and most of the time you can usually tell that it's a man in a dress. On the other hand, a transvestite is much more meticulous about her appearance." Here Trixie brushed her right hand through her hair as if for emphasis. "And she gets her kicks out of it too," she added provocatively.

"Kicks?"

"Sex," she said bluntly.

"But not this guy Joe?"

"No, he's straight as an arrow." Then she smiled. "Unless you hold his hobby against him."

"But," I said in further confusion, "you told me that all three of you came back here. I thought—"

"Joe just watched."

"Then Zack's—"

Trixie frowned. "Don't you dare say it. No, Zack's straight too. Just wanted to fool himself into thinkin' I'm a woman."

"That's sick," I said without thinking.

"If it doesn't harm you," she said angrily, "who are you to judge? Lots of straight guys come in here for the same thing. They'd never in a million years go to bed with another guy, but they come here, see a pretty girl in a beautiful dress, and somehow it's okay."

"But that doesn't make any sense," I objected, still struggling for an understanding, for some sort of a rational explanation.

"It's a trick," she said. "A trick they willin'ly let their minds play. It doesn't hurt them. It doesn't hurt me." She squared her shoulders. "I'm Trixie. I like being a woman, I'm good at it, and I enjoy it. And you better believe I make a helluva lot of money doin' it." She looked at me with open contempt. "Which reminds me, yours just ran out. I had fun with you for a little while, but now I'm tired of the game. You got more than you paid for. Your time is up."

With a flourish, Trixie whirled around on her heels and marched from the room, leaving me speechless in her wake. After a second, I remembered to close my mouth.

Still somewhat dazed by the unexpected turn of events, I looked down at my watch. It was almost three. I shook my head. What a night!

I wondered what Lee would say.

CHAPTER **FOURTEEN**

"Filled with comic lunacy,
this novel
is less a mystery
than
it's the Mad Hatter's Wild Ride
at Disneyland."

—Stokes Moran,
on Sarah Shankman's *The King Is Dead*

"*K*yle, you've got to tell the police," Lee said at the breakfast table the following morning, smearing a generous portion of orange marmalade on a piece of toast. I had just completed recounting for Lee the events of my previous night's visit to Tootsie's. The scrap of torn photograph and the matchbook lay inconspicuously on the tabletop between the salt and pepper shakers. "This time you don't have any choice."

"Tell them what?" I carefully sipped from my steaming mug of coffee. "I don't really have any hard evidence."

"You've got a name."

Zack. "Just a first name."

"And you've got a direct link between this hit man and a government official."

"That's just speculation. For all we know, Zack could have been a used-car salesman just here in town for a convention or something."

Lee gave me a quizzical look. "You know that's not true."

"Yeah, but I can't prove it."

"You don't have to prove anything. That's Lockwood's job. All you have to do is just tell him what you know."

I shook my head in disagreement. "Then he'll ask me how I know about all this stuff, and then where do you think I'll be?"

"Okay, so he may not be happy. But at least you'll have given him a couple of leads he might not otherwise have gotten—leads that in his hands might actually turn into something."

"Are you saying I'm a lousy investigator?"

"Not at all." She scooped more hash brown potatoes onto her plate. "It's just you don't have the resources Lockwood has."

"Resources?" I laughed. "Like what?"

"The FBI, state and local agencies, fingerprint files, mug shots, crime reports. Lockwood has a whole national network at his disposal."

"To do what?"

"Well, he—"

I shook my head again. "At this point, I can't even give Lockwood one solid piece of evidence. Everything I have is just pieced-together guesswork." I showed her my right hand and started listing off the items with my fingers. "One, I only think the man's name was Zack" (index finger), "two, I only think he was a hit man" (middle finger), "and three, I only think he met with a cop" (fourth finger). "He'll think I'm making it all up just to save my own scrawny neck."

"What about the matchbook?" Lee objected. "That's certainly hard evidence. You're not making that up. Trixie can verify it."

"Yes," I agreed, taking another sip of my coffee, "but where does that get us?"

"What do you mean?"

"According to Trixie, who claims she was with Zack every

minute he was at Tootsie's, the matchbook message was the only thing the least bit suspicious that passed between the two men."

"So?"

"So," I emphasized the conjunction, "the only thing in that matchbook is the single word Tipton."

"So? You live in Tipton. It's obvious the other man was giving Zack your address."

"Oh really?" I picked up the matchbook and flipped open the cover. "Where does it say that?"

"It's obvious."

"Is it? It's only obvious to us because we're trying to make a connection."

"I don't understand."

"How does the one word Tipton tell Zack anything?" I explained patiently. "There could be a hundred towns all across America named Tipton. Or, for all we know, it could be a person's name. Like J. Beresford Tipton, for instance."

"I see what you mean," Lee said, crumbling three bacon strips over her eggs.

"I'm not saying you're wrong," I continued. "As a matter of fact, I'm one hundred percent certain it's our Tipton. Otherwise it's all coincidence, and none of this makes any sense. But, if I was being fingered as we believe, then Zack needed more information than just that one word. He also needed a street address, not to mention what state it was in."

"You're right." Lee frowned in intense concentration. "Maybe Zack already knew the other details, and this guy Joe was merely confirming the location."

"Now you've lost me."

"Just bear with me for a minute," Lee said. "I'm thinking this out as I go along. Okay, how's this sound? Suppose the two men had previously talked over the phone, and Joe had given Zack several possible locations."

"Why?"

"Well, maybe he had uncovered a number of Kyle Malachis, and he might already have given Zack those addresses. So when Joe wrote out the one word, that was all the information Zack needed. What do you think of that?" She smiled in triumph.

"That's fine," I said. "As far as it goes."

"What do you mean, as far as it goes?"

"You're forgetting the bank card. According to Lockwood, it was issued ten months ago and mailed to my Tipton address. Wouldn't that seem to indicate that Zack already knew where I lived?"

"So?"

"Well, if he already knew where I lived, then what was the significance of Joe writing Tipton down in the matchbook? It had to have some import."

"Good point. Let me see." Lee cupped her chin, closing her eyes while she thought. Suddenly her eyes popped open. "Kyle, you travel a good bit."

"What's that got to do with anything?"

"Maybe Joe was just letting Zack know where you were. At the moment, you know. Instead of New York, or Los Angeles, or Louisville, this week, say, you're at home in Tipton, Connecticut. That's the reason for the one-word message Tipton. It lets Zack know everything he needs to know."

I nodded my head. "That does make sense. Okay, I'll buy that explanation. Good girl."

I reached for *The New York Times*, which still lay folded and unread on the tabletop next to my cereal bowl.

"I wonder if there's anything on the murder in the morning paper," I said as I snapped the pages open.

"Which murder?"

"Either one." Several pages into the Metro section, I found a three-inch story that boasted only a quarter-inch headline: TWO BODIES FOUND AT DOWNTOWN BUILDING.

"Here it is," I said.

"What does it say?"

I quickly scanned the article. "Not much. It says that papers found on the body led police at first to identify the victim as noted mystery critic Stokes Moran. But later information revealed that not to be the case. At present, the body is still unidentified. Uh-oh."

"What?"

"It says several hours later the body of Amy Torrence, age fifty-nine—I would have sworn she was eighty if she was a day—was found. She was also a victim of a knifing. Police don't yet know if the two crimes are related, but it says there is an eyewitness to the later killing." I let the newspaper fall into my lap. "Eyewitness." I looked into Lee's eyes. "Just who do you think it was this eyewitness may have seen? The killer? Or me?"

"Let's just hope it was the killer."

"Yeah, but with the way my luck's been running the last couple of days, you know which it will be."

"Does the article mention anything about the time Amy's body was found?"

"Just several hours later," I recounted from memory, then I lifted the newspaper for a double check. "No, you're right. It does give an exact time. Says the body was found around nine fifty-five."

Lee frowned. "Nine fifty-five? I'd say that was just about the time we left the scene."

"Are you sure?"

She shook her head. "Well, I wasn't keeping a stopwatch on it, no. But I'd have to guess we were down there sometime between nine-thirty and ten."

"If that eyewitness did indeed spot me, don't you think Lockwood would have been knocking down our door by this time?"

"I don't know. Kyle"—Lee reached across the table and grabbed my hand—"now more than ever, you've got to talk to the police. And tell them everything."

I lifted her hand to my lips and kissed it. She smiled and drew it back to her cheek. Then I stood up.

"Where are you going?"

"Down to see Lockwood."

"Good."

I smiled, shaking my head. "Don't get your hopes up. I'm just going to get my money clip back."

I left Lee frowning into her oatmeal.

The doorman on duty downstairs this morning was not the same one as last night. If Lee's building conformed to normal eight-hour shifts, I suppose three doormen were employed overall, but I had never seen more than two—Marco and Felipe. So now I handed Marco a twenty-dollar bill, explaining that it was in repayment for a taxi fare, and asked him to please return it with my thanks to Felipe when the other man came on duty. He said he would be happy to oblige. Well, Marco, I thought as I headed out the door, let's just see how honest you really are. Tonight, I'll make it a point to ask Felipe if he indeed received the money.

Outside, the day was simply majestic. There was just no other word for it. It was the kind of morning that the New York City Convention and Visitors Bureau loves—sun shining brightly, temperature hovering somewhere around a very pleasant sixty degrees Fahrenheit, breeze slight if detectable at all, visibility clear for miles, not a cloud anywhere in the sky. October can truly be the best month in the Big Apple.

I stood for a moment on the sidewalk, debating whether to take the Land Rover or hail a cab. About a foot to my left, the sidewalk exploded. At first I thought a marble had been dropped from one of the upper floors, but when a second explosion hit the brick wall behind me, I realized what was happening. Dropping into a protective crouch, I scuttled back to the relative safety of the doorway, then turned and looked back out at the street.

The doorman, now also adopting a similar crouch, crawled toward me.

"What's going on?" Marco whispered in alarm.

"Somebody's shooting."

"In this neighborhood? This is crazy."

"You got that right." From my limited vantage point, I continued to scan the cars and buildings across the street, hoping to catch at least a glimpse of the sniper, but I saw nothing. "And I'll tell you something even crazier."

"What's that?"

"They were shooting at me."

CHAPTER **FIFTEEN**

"Writers
with axes to grind
against various and sundry
societal ills
have incorporated their causes
in their mysteries
since the days
of Conan Doyle and Wilkie Collins."

—Stokes Moran,
on Alan Russell's *The Forest Prime Evil*

I remained downstairs until the first blue-and-white police unit arrived on the scene.

"What's this world coming to?" the doorman had asked after I had placed the 911 call on the house phone next to his cubicle.

"Good question," I said.

Once the initial danger had passed, with no further bullets being fired, no terrorists storming the front of the building, and no hand grenades being lobbed, my knees started to quiver, and I slid down on the cold tile with my back propped against the wall.

Someone had tried to kill me. It took a minute for the import of that statement to hit home. The game had now become real. It was no longer a simple mind exercise, with abstract victims and killers. The bogus Stokes Moran, even the flesh-and-blood Amy, had not quite elevated my personal apprehension for my own safety beyond a bearable threshold. It was one thing to talk with Lee about a possible hit man, surmise his intentions, interpret his actions, but it was quite another finally to realize it really was my name on the bullet, my skull in the crosshairs of a sniper's gun. The reality stunned me.

I sat on my hands to keep Marco from seeing how badly they were shaking. By the time the police arrived, I had collapsed to an almost fetal position.

"Who made the call?" a uniformed woman asked as she and her male partner entered the foyer. The policewoman topped five feet ten at least and weighed close to one hundred and seventy pounds. Like her physical presence, her tone allowed no room for misinterpretation.

"I did," I said.

"You Kyle Malachi?" She pronounced it Malicky.

"Yes."

"I'm Officer Herndon." She then nodded in the direction of the other policeman, a Hispanic-looking man who was both shorter and stockier than his partner. "And this is Officer Wilson. We're responding to a nine-one-one call where you said somebody shot at you?"

"That's right." I walked with her outside and pointed to the chip in the sidewalk where the first bullet had struck. I then added that another bullet had hit the wall somewhere behind where I had been standing.

"Did you see the gunman?"

"No."

"Did anyone else see the gunman?"

"I don't know," I said. "I don't think so."

While Officer Herndon stayed with me and continued writing out a report, her partner scoured the front of the building for the second bullet hole.

"I found it," he shouted after a couple of minutes. He

reached in his pocket and pulled out a penknife, with which he removed the bullet from the wall.

"Looks like a twenty-two," he said, open-palming it for Herndon's inspection.

"Looks like you were right," Herndon said to me, giving no indication that her statement sounded like a disbelieving challenge. "Were there any other witnesses to the shooting?"

"Marco heard the shots, I think," I answered. On one hand, I appreciated Herndon's businesslike manner. But, on the other, there were certain aspects of her officious demeanor that came close to being downright insulting. I decided, since I would never ask her out on a date, it was a personality trait that I could tolerate. Under the present circumstances.

"Who's Marco?"

"He's the doorman." I nodded in Marco's direction.

While Officer Herndon finished up with me, getting such vital information as my full name, my address, my telephone number, and my occupation, Officer Wilson went to interview Marco.

Poor Marco was still being questioned when Herndon finally dismissed me and graciously allowed that I could now return to my apartment upstairs. As I waited for the elevator, I watched Marco's animated theatrics with Officer Wilson. He was in the middle of what I could only interpret as his blow-by-blow account of the shooting when the elevator arrived. The last I glimpsed of Marco, he had dropped to a crouch and was duck-stepping toward the front door.

What do I tell Lee? I thought as I rode up the seventeen floors. Tell her the truth, and risk frightening her, or say nothing, and field her wrath when she finds out, which she inevitably will? Several tenants had observed my encounter with the police.

Tell her, I decided as I opened the door and called out her name, alerting her to my return.

"That was a quick trip. You surely didn't make it all the way downtown and get back so fast."

"I didn't," I admitted. "I never left the building." I then proceeded to inform her of everything that had transpired in the past forty-five minutes.

"Kyle, are you all right?" she asked as I finished the recital of events.

"Yeah, just a little wobbly."

"You've got to tell Lockwood everything now. You can't put it off any longer."

"If I tell him, I could end up behind bars."

"And if you don't, you could end up six feet under. Now which do you prefer?"

"All right, I'll give him a call."

I asked Lee for Lockwood's card and punched in the number. It was answered on the third ring.

"Sixth Precinct, Detective Jeffers speaking." It was a woman's voice.

"Detective Lockwood, please."

"I'm sorry. He's not in at the moment. Would you like to leave a message?"

What should I say? Yeah, I'm the guy who removed evidence from the scene of Amy's murder. Yeah, I'm also the one who didn't report her death. Or yeah, I'm the real Stokes Moran, the man currently at the top of the mob's hit list. Instead, I merely said a polite "No, thank you" and hung up.

"Well?" Lee asked when I joined her in the kitchen.

"He wasn't in."

"Did you leave a message for him to call you back when he returned?"

"I'll call him later."

"Kyle." In Lee's wifely tone, she managed to turn my name into an admonition.

"I will." I held up two fingers to my forehead in a mock Scout salute. "I promise."

"All right." She poked me in the ribs as I squeezed a path between her chair and the cupboard. "But you better."

I stood at the sink, looking out the window at the bare back wall of the building next door. I then turned around and watched as Lee busied herself leafing through a magazine at the kitchen table. For once, there was not a scrap of food in sight.

"What are you doing?" I asked absently.

"Looking for recipes." She glanced up just in time to catch my grin. "What are you thinking?" she teased.

"Nothing."

"Admit it, you think I'm getting fat."

"Not at all."

"Don't give me that. I saw your smirk."

"I don't know what you're talking about."

She laughed. "Okay, just for that, we'll both go on a diet after the baby comes."

"Fine by me," I answered, then lapsed into silence, turning once again to look out the window. What was going on? Why couldn't I make sense out of it? Who was behind it all?

"Kyle, say something."

"I don't have a clue," I finally said.

"You can't figure out every mystery," she said, uncannily reading my thoughts.

"There must be something I'm missing, something that should be staring me in the face."

Lee pushed back the chair and walked over to where I was standing. "You can't expect real life to always mimic the pages of a mystery novel. Some puzzles just can't be figured out."

"Somehow I don't agree," I said. "I've read literally thousands of mysteries in my lifetime, and I just don't believe there are any new plots left. Since the time of Edgar Allan Poe, the most fertile and creative minds in the business have applied every conceivable twist, turn, zig, and zag in devising some of the most fiendishly clever puzzles ever concocted. Wife killers, husband killers, mama killers, papa killers, kid killers, serial killers, evil scientists, imperiled heroines—it's all been done. Writers may come up with different spins maybe, but basically nothing totally brand new has come along since the Bible."

"In that case, I'm sure you'll pull something out of that Mystery Gazetteer you keep locked away in your head."

"I wish." I turned to look her in the face. "If we just had some suspects."

She laughed. "Well, are there any mystery novels like that?"

"I can't think of a one." I joined the laughter. "I've read novels where all the suspects were guilty, where all the suspects were innocent, where all the suspects died, and many where either the most likely suspect or the least likely suspect turned out to be the guilty party. But I can't think of a single mystery that I've ever read where there were absolutely no suspects."

"Until this one."

"Yeah." I curled my left arm around her shoulder. "It's just too bad that this one's not a book. At least then I could skip ahead to the last page and see who did it."

"Kyle, you wouldn't! You'd never commit such a sacrilege." She paused. "Would you?"

"If it would help me figure this thing out, you better bet I would." I dropped my arm from around her shoulder and turned to face her. "In a heartbeat," I said as I planted a kiss on the tip of her nose for emphasis. I then pressed my lips against hers.

"Mmm, tell me more," she murmured as she wrapped her arms around my waist.

Just then the doorbell rang. I reluctantly disengaged from my wife's embrace and squinted through the peephole to see just what idiot we had to thank for some incredibly bad timing.

It was Lockwood.

CHAPTER SIXTEEN

"Although the situations
are patently absurd,
the reader
nevertheless gets caught up
in the tension of the
moment."

—Stokes Moran,
on Sharyn McCrumb's *Missing Susan*

"*I* just happened to overhear the dispatch on the police band," Lockwood explained as I ushered him through the hallway and into the living room. "Then when they gave this address, I knew it had to be you, even though they got the name all wrong."

Yeah—Malicky, I bet.

"Please sit down," I said, indicating the sofa. I picked a chair opposite him on the other side of the coffee table. "So you already know what happened? The shooting and all?"

"Yeah." Lockwood perched on the edge of the cushion, his gangly knees towering awkwardly four inches above the level of the seat. "I ran into Officers Herndon and Wilson downstairs. They filled me in."

"Then don't you think this proves that Kyle has been a target all along?" Lee said, suddenly materializing in the doorway.

Lockwood jerked to his feet. "That certainly is a possibility."

"What else could it be?" she asked.

"I don't know. That's what I'm here to find out."

"You don't think for a minute that Kyle shot at himself? Do you?"

Lockwood grinned a half-smile. "I didn't say that, but there's a lot going on with you people that just doesn't track."

"What do you mean?" I asked nervously, fearful he had somehow connected me with Amy's murder. The eyewitness? Had I been identified after all?

He spoke. "Well, to start with, you publicly announce the death of your . . . what did you call it?" He fumbled for the word.

"Pseudonym," Lee volunteered.

"Yeah, well, that's weird enough right there—announcing the death of your other self or something." I felt blood flushing my cheeks. "Then, a real stiff turns up with this pseudo whatever's name, including real and fake IDs. I gotta tell you, right from the start, I knew this one was going to be trouble."

"We explained why Kyle did that," Lee said. "Didn't you believe us?"

"Oh, yeah. Every single word." Lockwood laughed, then added, "Because at the time, it seemed too ridiculous not to believe."

I frowned. "You said 'at the time.' Has something since happened to change your mind?"

"It's just the longer this goes, the crazier it gets." Lockwood walked over to the window. "An assistant U.S. attorney gets involved"—here he turned back to face us—"then the FBI calls—"

"FBI?" I said. "You didn't tell me that."

"I haven't talked to you since it happened." Lockwood stopped, then jammed both hands into his front pants pockets. When he didn't immediately continue, I demanded, "Well, what did they want?"

"It was a guy I know, a New York field agent. I'll keep his name out of it for the moment. Well, he called up and said he thought they had a pretty good idea who my John Doe might be. Then he asked if I'd turn the case over to them."

"Turn it over to the FBI?" I echoed.

"Yeah."

"What did you say?" Lee was as eager as I to find out his answer.

"I asked him what was going on, then I suggested why don't we work together. You know, interagency cooperation and all that."

"And?" Lee and I said the word together.

Lockwood walked toward the chair where I was sitting. He looked me straight in the eyes. "He told me he couldn't do that. That I would just have to trust him on this."

I gulped. "Gummint" killers? I remembered Amy's descriptive word. Had I inadvertently stumbled into some sort of government conspiracy? Could this be another Watergate? And where were Woodward and Bernstein when you needed them?

"And did you?" I finally found the courage to ask. "Trust him, I mean?"

"No, I didn't." Lockwood abruptly dropped his gaze from my eyes and reclaimed his perch on the sofa.

A puzzled frown crossed my wife's face. "What are you trying to tell us?"

Lockwood leaned back against the sofa's cushions. "I really don't know. And on top of everything else that's happened, now there's a sniper gunning for you." With his eyes, he transformed the statement into a question.

"You think I know something?" I said, shifting uneasily in my chair.

"Yes, I do. Everything seems to revolve around you."

"Kyle," Lee prodded. I knew she was trying to urge me to spill my guts, to tell him about Amy and Zack and Tootsie's and all the rest. I still wasn't sure he wouldn't lock me in a cell and throw away the key. He never once mentioned Amy. Maybe he hadn't made the connection after all? Maybe he wasn't even the detective assigned to Amy's murder?

"Kyle," Lee repeated, interrupting my thoughts. "Tell him."

I debated the pros and cons. I could feel my wife's eyes boring into my head. Lockwood sat mute, waiting expectantly. Finally, I capitulated.

"All right." I told him everything.

"Am I under arrest?"

He laughed. "No, not unless there's a law on the books against stupidity."

I felt insulted, but Lee joined in with Lockwood's laughter.

"I sure do know one thing, though. I'da given a whole month's pay just to have seen that striptease. It musta been something else." His laughter became even more animated. So did Lee's.

"It was a sight to behold," she confirmed. "I wish I had it on videotape."

Their easy camaraderie at my expense further offended my already damaged ego. "Well, I'm glad you're both so amused."

"Oh, Kyle," Lee said, trying to squelch her giggling, and failing. "It's funny. Admit it."

I forced a smile I didn't feel. "Yeah. Real hilarious."

"I'm sorry, Mr. Malachi," Lockwood said, successfully quelling his laughter but unable to suppress a smile. "But this is one story that's going to keep me in drinks for a year." I could just imagine him and his cronies down at the local pub, with me the butt of their infantile jokes. On second thought, bad choice of words.

"At least a year," he added.

"So you didn't know anything about Amy's death?" I asked, trying to steer the conversation back to less personal areas.

Lockwood shook his head. "It's not my case. Of course, I'd heard another body had turned up at the same location, but I don't think anybody ever connected the two."

"Why not?" I asked. "Weren't both Zack and Amy knifed?"

"Seems so, from what you tell me," he said. "But this latest vic was a bag lady."

"So?" Lee challenged, her politically correct antenna sensing discrimination.

"No, no," Lockwood said. I had to credit him, he hadn't missed the obvious disdain in my wife's voice. "You misunderstand me. It's that these street people are always getting mugged, usually by one another. I can assure you her death will be fully investigated. What I meant was simply that we wouldn't automatically link the two killings."

"But why not?" Lee continued. "Both were killed in the same manner and at the same place and within less than twenty-four hours of each other. That sounds like a connection to me."

Lockwood nodded. "After what your husband just told me, I'll definitely look into it."

But Lee was not ready to concede the point. "Why does what Kyle just told you make any difference whatsoever?" Lee pushed herself up from the sofa. "It's obvious to me that one pitiful old bag lady isn't as important to the New York City Police Department as some unidentified white man who's probably no better than a hired thug." She stalked from the room. Lockwood jumped to his feet, a look of concern on his face.

"Don't mind my wife," I said, trying to cover the awkward silence Lee's sudden departure created. But I don't mind admitting that I couldn't help feeling just a little bit pleased that Lockwood's FedEx pursuit of my wife had hit an unexpected bump in the road.

"What did I say?" he asked, shrugging palms up in a gesture of perplexity.

"It's not you. Lee just has a hard time avoiding the truth."

Lockwood frowned, and I wondered if I had perhaps said too much. But the detective's only response was an all-encompassing "women."

I agreed with Lee. If nothing else, murder should at least create a final equality for its victims. Any investigation into a violent or unnatural death shouldn't bend to the status of a person's life, only at the matter and manner of the killing—democracy at its purest, so to speak. I was proud of my wife not only for her personal sensitivity but also for her unfortunately correct perception. Amy deserved better than a routine ink swipe on some pompous bureaucrat's official form. In triplicate. Hopefully now she would get it.

"You ready to go downtown?" Lockwood abruptly asked, heading out into the hallway.

"What?" I was rudely jolted back to reality. "You told me only a few minutes ago that you weren't going to arrest me."

"I'm not arresting you. But I need you to come down to the station house and sign a statement."

"A statement?"

He nodded. "Yeah. It's very simple. All we do is just put everything you told me down in writing."

"Everything?"

He smiled. "Yes, everything."

"Couldn't I do that here?"

"No," he said. "Look. It's no big deal. You'll be finished in an hour. Tops."

I reluctantly agreed—but who was I kidding? I knew I really didn't have a choice—then went to tell Lee of my imminent departure.

"I feel like such a fool," she said, digging through the

refrigerator. "Making such a scene. What that poor man must think."

"That poor man doesn't know what hit him," I answered affectionately. "And besides, you were right."

She pulled out a jar of pickles. I stooped and quickly kissed her lips while they were still undilled. Then I returned to Lockwood.

But he had already left the apartment. I found him standing out in the foyer, waiting for the elevator. The sliding steel door had just creaked open as I reached his side.

"You want to ride downtown with me?" he asked as we stepped into the narrow cubicle.

I remembered the sound of the bullets, the marblelike explosion on the sidewalk, the cringing in the doorway. Then I pictured the comforting security of the police cruiser, the protective glass, the wire cage, an experienced and trained detective serving as a bodyguard. No unknown sniper would be able to reach me, no piercing bullet seek me out. I would be safe.

"Besides," he added, "it'll give us more of a chance to talk."

That's what I was afraid of. "I'll take my own car," I answered quickly.

CHAPTER **SEVENTEEN**

"With just a dash of whimsy
and a pinch of parody,
the author
brings to life
an endearing and enduring character
in whose welcome company
readers take pleasure and delight."

—Stokes Moran,
on Simon Brett's *Mrs. Pargeter's Package*

"*I*'ll only be a couple of minutes," I said as the elevator jolted to a stop on the first floor.

"I'll wait out front," Lockwood answered, stepping out into the lobby. "It's the blue Oldsmobile."

"White Land Rover," I called as the door closed behind him. I exited the elevator at the garage level and walked over to where Lee's car was parked.

The underground garage was one of the good things about this building. In Manhattan, parking was at such a premium some people actually prized their parking spaces more than their own lives, as recent headlines could attest. I recalled the details of the story because it had struck me as so ridiculous and so New York. Both the *Post*—MAN KILLED OVER PARKING DISPUTE—and *Newsday*—BROKERS' SCUFFLE ENDS IN DEATH—had devoted front-page coverage to the bizarre tale. It seemed two junior partners in a Wall Street investment firm had quarreled over which one would inherit a parking space in the event one of the senior partners retired. What had started out as more or less a teasing verbal exchange had soon escalated into heated anger, physical violence, and then outrageous murder. The irony turned out to be that none of the senior partners were even contemplating retirement anytime this century. Talk about being bullish on America, this was definitely Emma Lathen territory.

Steering the Land Rover up the ramp and out onto the street, I spotted Lockwood sitting behind the wheel of a midnight-blue Cutlass Ciera. I should have realized that a plain-clothes detective would correspondingly drive an unmarked car. I honked the horn, and he pulled out ahead of me.

Trying to follow a lead car through the streets of New York City is no easy task, not even on an early Saturday afternoon when traffic is admittedly lighter than during the week. From time to time Lockwood would change lanes, usually to skirt around double-parked vehicles, sometimes to pass slow-moving tourists. Twice I had to speed up to make a yellow light before it turned red, and three times impatient taxi drivers squeezed in between us. But throughout the long obstacle course that was Lockwood's route downtown, I never once lost visual contact with the Ciera. Finally he turned left off a side street and into a fenced-in parking area, motioning for me to pull my car in alongside his.

"You sure I won't get towed?" I asked as I stepped out of the Land Rover.

"No problem," he answered, hurriedly scribbling on a little writing pad he had only a second earlier retrieved from inside his jacket. "But I'm going to leave this note on your windshield just in case."

We then walked over to a side door that warned POLICE PERSONNEL ONLY. Opening the door and ducking under the low overhang, Lockwood led me through a maze of hallways, all conspicuously indistinct in that drab government green that must surely be the result of some national conspiracy, since every federal, state, and local facility that I've ever entered seems to sport that same god-awful color. Then up two narrow flights of carpetless stairs, and finally into a newsroom-style office whose noise and chaos would give even the New York Stock Exchange a run for its money.

"Have a seat." He indicated a vacant chair next to an empty desk. "I'm going to arrange for a stenographer, then I'll see if we can borrow the captain's office."

Five minutes later Lockwood returned. "Everything's all set," he said. "My captain's out to lunch."

"Figuratively or literally?"

"Huh?"

"Forget it." I followed him across the room and into an enclosed cubicle. A slim and extremely attractive brunette was already seated behind the desk. She smiled as I entered.

"Ms. Krupinski here will type out your statement," Lockwood explained. "Please remember to spell all proper names and addresses. Once you're finished, you'll get a chance to look it over and make whatever corrections, deletions, or additions you deem necessary. Then sign it, and you can be on your way." The words weren't quite as rote-driven as a Miranda warning, but they still sounded like oft-repeated copspeak.

"As simple as that?" I still didn't quite trust him not to throw me in a cell.

"As simple as that."

And surprisingly it was. Lockwood occasionally interrupted with either a question or a clarification. But basically I gave Ms. Krupinski a straightforward account of everything that had happened to me in the last forty-eight hours.

After signing the statement, I walked with Lockwood back to his desk.

"Do you have any leads in the case?" I asked, taking a seat in the visitor's chair next to the desk.

He shook his head. "Basically just what you already know, that the feds are somehow involved, which your information reinforces. I guess I'll have to find out who this guy Joe really is. It sounds to me like he might be the key."

"Do you think it's some kind of a cover-up or conspiracy?"

"To be honest, I don't know what to think, but," he added with a smile, "I do believe I'll pay a little visit to Tootsie's myself."

"What about Amy?"

"Oh, don't worry, I haven't forgotten about her. I just haven't yet had a chance to check with the detective in charge," he said. "With Pride gone, I've had all I could handle just with my own cases." As if for emphasis, he then glanced down at the dozen or so files that lay scattered across the top of his desk, spreading his hands in a sweeping gesture.

"By the way," I asked, "where is your partner?"

"Oh, he had a family wedding or something. Seems like every Saturday we're scheduled, he comes up with some excuse to be absent."

"You don't work every weekend?"

"Good Lord, no. One in four is bad enough. If I had to give up all my Saturdays, believe me, I'd turn in my badge. Especially during college basketball season."

I grinned. "You look like a basketball player."

"I was. Made All-Conference my junior and senior years."

"Which conference?"

"The Ivy League." He answered almost sheepishly.

Lockwood hadn't struck me as much of a scholar, let alone an Ivy Leaguer. "Which school?" I asked, impressed in spite of myself.

He was somewhat hesitant with his answer. "Princeton," he finally said. I had indeed underestimated my adversary.

But enough of this male bonding. Why was I continuing to converse with this man? It wasn't as if I was actually starting to like him. Or was it?

"Am I free to go?" I asked abruptly.

"Sure. Now that we have your statement, you're as free as a bird."

What kind of bird? I wondered. Lark? Or jailbird? Lockwood had still revealed very little about the case. By this time, he certainly had received the autopsy results. But he never said a word. Should I ask? Or would he interpret my curiosity as a sign of guilt? I remained wary of his motivations despite his outwardly friendly demeanor. He might be waiting for just one last piece to the puzzle before bringing out the handcuffs. I decided to press the issue.

"Does that mean I'm also free to leave town?"

He frowned, and paused for a moment before answering. "I suppose there's no problem with that. You'll be going back to your place in Connecticut?"

I stood up. "As fast as modern transportation can carry me."

He nodded his head. "Well then, I guess that means I'll need to contact the Tipton police."

"Whatever for?"

"Have you forgotten that somebody took a couple of potshots at you this morning? It won't be quite the same as if you had remained in the city, where I could have seen to your safety myself, but it shouldn't be all that difficult to arrange for the Tipton authorities to keep you under surveillance until this matter is settled."

Surveillance? "I don't want any police protection," I protested hurriedly. I certainly didn't want the Tipton police shadowing my every move and reporting back to Lockwood. I wanted to be rid of him and the threat he posed once and for all. I'd rather take my chances with the unknown sniper.

"It's just routine. For your own protection."

I stubbornly shook my head. "No, not for me. I don't want it."

For an instant, Lockwood's eyes locked with mine, then he

abruptly dropped his gaze. "Okay then, suit yourself. If you feel that strongly about it, I won't force the issue." Somehow to my ears Lockwood's words lacked believability, or maybe it was merely my suspicious nature. Either way, I had the feeling I'd be looking over my shoulder for quite some time to come.

"Well, at least I'll know how to reach you. If I need to, of course." His grin followed me all the way out the door.

"Damn." I was halfway back to the apartment before I realized I hadn't asked Lockwood to return my money clip. "And I was hoping I'd seen the last of him," I said aloud in the car.

But somehow, even as I was walking out of the precinct house, I had experienced the eerie sensation that Lockwood was still watching me, still dogging my steps. I didn't quite accept his dismissal as final.

Mainly because there were just too many holes left in the case. Had Lockwood been totally truthful when he had told me he knew nothing about Amy's murder? Don't detectives normally talk about their cases among themselves? At the time, it had seemed somewhat disingenuous on Lockwood's part not to express any interest whatsoever in another body being found in the same location. Now it seemed positively ominous. You'd think he'd at least discuss the coincidence with his fellow detectives, just to rule out a connection, if for no other reason. Plus the newspaper had mentioned an eyewitness. Did Lockwood already know that the eyewitness would identify me? Was he lulling me into a false sense of security, hoping I'd make some kind of careless, self-incriminating mistake?

As if the stupid blunders I'd made thus far weren't sufficient. This case was truly one for the books—the "How Not To" books. Every desperate attempt I'd made in the last two days to extricate myself from the suction of suspicion had only dragged me deeper into the mire. Was I finally free of the quicksand, or just blindly sinking deeper than ever before?

And the most important question of all—how far could Lock-wood be trusted?

I needed to talk to Lee. True, earlier today she'd lost a little of her regard for Lockwood, which, as far as I was concerned, was all to the good. But I decided she'd still be able to give me her honest assessment of this turn of events—whether I was truly exonerated or rightly paranoid?

I left the Land Rover with the garage attendant, then took the elevator up to the seventeenth floor. As I approached the apartment door, I realized that very shortly I'd be standing in front of another door, this one to my own house in Tipton. The forced two-day banishment had seemed more like two months. As secure and comforting as Lee's apartment had been, it still wasn't home. It lacked the essentials—Bootsie and Wee. Suddenly I was overcome with an urgent desire to hold those two dear animals in my arms and rub my face against their fur.

I jammed the key in the lock, calling out to my wife even as I disengaged the bolt and swung open the door.

"Lee, guess what? We can go home."

Hearing no immediate response, I walked through the silent rooms eager to find my wife and share with her the news of our release.

"Lee?" I continued to call her name, first in the hallway, then in the living room, the dining room, the kitchen, the bedroom.

"Lee, where are you?" By the time I had reached the bathroom, I was becoming a little bit anxious.

"Lee?" I repeated as I retraced my steps through the apartment. I couldn't imagine where she had gone. After all, she didn't have access to a car. I had taken the Land Rover with me down to Lockwood's office. Lee almost never took taxis or buses. And I also doubted that she would have gone out for a walk or to the market knowing that I might return at any minute. If nothing else, her curiosity would have glued her here.

Just in case, though, I checked several places where she might conceivably have left a note—inside the front door, the top of the credenza, her pillow on the bed, the outside of the refrigerator. Nothing.

Finally I picked up the phone. "Marco," I said when he answered, "it's Kyle Malachi. By any chance, have you seen my wife?"

"Yeah, she left about half an hour ago."

Left? I couldn't believe it, this wasn't like Lee at all—to just up and leave without explanation. "Did she say where she was going?"

"No. Nobody said a thing."

"Nobody? You mean someone else was with her?"

"Oh, sure," he said. "Two men."

"Two men? Had you ever seen them before?"

"No, I can't say that I have. But she must have known them. She let them up."

"Let them up?"

"Yeah," he said with a nod. "I called, gave her their names, and she said send them up."

"You know their names!" I exclaimed. "Why didn't you tell me?"

Marco shook his head. "I'm sorry. I just can't remember their names. You know, it was only for a minute, and I forgot what they'd told me almost as soon as they were on the elevator."

"That's okay," I said, not really meaning it, then changed tactics. "By any chance did you happen to notice when they all came back down if my wife appeared to go with them willingly?" I tried to keep the rising panic out of my voice, but was obviously failing.

"What do you mean?" I could hear the suspicious alarm in Marco's words and understood exactly what he must be thinking—had he somehow been derelict in his duty, had he unknowingly failed to protect one of his tenants? I also realized that if he started feeling guilty, I'd never get a straight answer.

I deliberately calmed my tone. "I was just wondering if they were old friends or something."

"I don't know," he said, and I could tell that at least for the moment I had successfully managed to curb his uneasiness. "Everything seemed fine to me."

"Can you tell me anything about the two men? What they looked like? You know, something that might help me figure out where my wife's gotten herself off to." I hoped that to Marco my concern seemed almost casual, like a husband just a little bit irritated with a forgetful wife who'd failed to leave a note as to where she was going.

"The men were just wearing regular business suits, like the kind I see every day. Nothing remarkable that I could tell."

"How were they acting? Did everything seem to be on friendly terms?" What I really wanted to know was if Lee had been forced to accompany the two men at gunpoint, but I couldn't very well put it to Marco like that.

"I guess so. One of the men was holding Miss Holland's left arm by the elbow, but she didn't seem to mind."

"So Lee wasn't protesting? She went along with them willingly?" Yeah, probably with a .45 poking her in the ribs.

"It sure looked that way to me."

"Did you notice which direction they took when they left the building?"

"They didn't take any direction," he said simply. "They just got into a car and drove away."

"You mean they left the car in front of the building while they went up to get Lee?" Such an action was risky, especially if somebody wanted to avoid notice. Parking on this street usually guaranteed an immediate tow, even on a Saturday. Except for Lee, of course, who seemingly had a guardian angel somewhere deep inside the New York City Bureau of Traffic Control.

"No," Marco answered. "The car pulled up to the curb as soon as they walked out."

That meant there was a third man involved. I remembered that Amy had also mentioned three men—two men had disposed of the body, while a third man had remained behind the wheel. The similarities were too striking to be coincidental. Not good, I decided, not good at all.

"Could you tell anything about the car? What kind it was? What year? What color? The tag number?" I knew I was pushing too hard, and I prayed that Marco wouldn't hear the frantic anxiety in my voice.

"Just that it was a black sedan," he said, then added a little bit defensively, "You know, with all the rich cars around here, I don't pay much attention to exact makes or models."

"Was it a rich car?" I asked, borrowing his archaic description.

He shook his head. "Nah, I don't think so. Probably just middle class. But I can't be sure."

"That's all right," I said, trying to reassure him. "You did fine, Marco. Thanks for the help."

"Oh," he said, "I just remembered something else. I don't know if it means anything, but Miss Holland asked me not to forget to water her plants. Like it's not something I already do twice a week."

Water her plants? The request sounded so ridiculous, so utterly normal that it didn't make sense. It was something you'd ask before you left on vacation. Did that mean Lee knew even then that she wouldn't be coming back anytime soon? More than anything else Marco had volunteered, this admission scared me the most. So why hadn't Lee put up a struggle? Kicked and clawed and dug in her heels? Screamed bloody murder? Come on, get real, Kyle. Your wife's seven months pregnant, for crissakes. She was obviously protecting the baby.

I thanked Marco again and disconnected the call. Staring unblinkingly into space, and trying to slow the out-of-control jackhammer in my chest, I finally translated my fear into two tangible and concrete thoughts, then faced the undeniable and terrifying reality they represented.

My wife was missing.

And what's worse, I had ample reason to believe she'd been kidnapped.

CHAPTER **EIGHTEEN**

*"As the intrepid sleuth
chips away at the puzzle,
someone is watching
who feels absolutely no
compunction about removing obstacles,
not even a pregnant
woman."*

—Stokes Moran,
on Leslie Meier's *Tippy-Toe Murder*

*L*ee was missing!

That was the only thing I could think about. Nothing else mattered. I no longer cared whether Lockwood suspected me of murder, I was no longer interested in who might have killed Amy or the John Doe in the morgue, and above all I could care less about my infantile jealousy of Stokes Moran. The only thing that meant anything to me at this moment was Lee, and getting her back safe and unharmed.

I couldn't breathe.

Everything was my fault. I had pursued this case with a reckless disregard for anything except my own ego. Lee had warned me to let the police handle the investigation. But I had stubbornly refused to listen. Now I had placed Lee's life in jeopardy. Who had taken her? Where had they taken her? And, most important, why had they taken her? If I could find the answer to that last question, perhaps the other questions would answer themselves.

I knew I had to act fast, but what should I do? What could I do?

As if by instinct, I picked up the phone and called Nolan. Yes, I thought, Nolan. God bless him, he'll be able to help, tell me what to do, give me some direction.

"Damn!" I said. The line was busy. Why had I never added Call Waiting to my phone service? It was too late now.

Next I tried Lockwood. Any port in a storm, right?

"Answer, dammit!" The phone rang six, seven times. Finally somebody picked up. Sighing gratefully, I asked for Lockwood.

"He's away from his desk," the female voice responded.

"He was there less than an hour ago," I complained impatiently.

"Well, I'm sorry, but he's not here now. Would you care to leave a message?"

"No, I would not care to leave a message," I mimicked irritably, and hung up.

I cupped my hands over my chin and shook my head back and forth. Think, Kyle, think. I tried Nolan again. This time I slammed the receiver down with frustration.

"Damn busy signal!"

Suddenly I felt claustrophobic. I had to act, to move, to do something, anything. But first I had to get out of this apartment where everything reminded me of Lee—the open sack of Chips Ahoy on the credenza, the spilled canister of Pringles on the coffee table, the empty olive jar on the sofa. The sense of loss was suffocating and overwhelming.

"I haven't lost anything," I shouted defiantly to the walls as I ran to the door. "Lee will be fine."

The elevator took forever, then Marco wasn't at his post when I arrived downstairs. He had closed and locked the front door for security, so anyone would need a key to get in.

"He's probably out walking Mrs. Carstairs's dogs again," I muttered. I had wanted to leave a message with him, on the off chance that Lee suddenly returned or telephoned. But it probably would have been a wasted effort. If what I feared was true, I doubted that Lee would be inquiring for messages anytime soon.

What would I have said in the message anyway? "I've gone out to look for you." "Stay put until I get back." "Call me when you get in." None of those possibilities seemed remotely sensible.

As I approached the driver's side of the Land Rover, I decided it was about time I caught up with the rest of the world and joined the communications age. If nothing else, I was going to get a car phone. Right then, a cellular telephone would have proved absolutely indispensable. But I doubted if even Ma Bell herself could have managed to get one installed and operational on a Saturday afternoon. In Manhattan, no less.

I pulled out of the underground garage with no clear plan of action and no idea of where I was going. I looked at my watch. It was one minute shy of four-thirty. Only two days ago at almost this precise time, I had made that fateful call to *The New York Times.* Just forty-eight hours, and yet in that short period of time my whole comfortable universe had totally disintegrated. Do human beings always live so near to utter disaster? Are we blithely unaware of how constantly close the precipice remains? Is there no safety net, no cushion, no protection from one false step? Obviously not. If only I could turn back the clock and undo the damage of the last two days. Lee, where are you? Please be safe. If anything happens to you, I'll never forgive myself.

I braked for the traffic signal at West 116th Street and Lenox Avenue. What was I doing here? I had no memory of making the turns necessary to arrive at this point; in fact, I had no memory of anything since leaving Lee's apartment building on West Eighty-second Street. Where did I think I was going? Then the realization hit me. This was the route I normally took when I'd head back to Tipton after a visit to the city. Subconsciously, I must have made the decision to go home.

I can't do that, I chided myself. I need to turn this car around and stay in Manhattan so I can find Lee, start a search for her, be nearby when she's found. The light changed, and I continued straight ahead on Lenox.

Maybe it wasn't such a bad idea to go home, after all. At least it would give me an opportunity to talk with Nolan face to face. In the past, whenever I had found myself in need of police assistance, Nolan had always proved a tremendous ally, a blessed go-between, a reliable shortcut. But today my need was greater than ever. I suddenly acknowledged how desperately I wanted Nolan's counsel, his experience, his presence. He was more than an ex-cop or a next-door neighbor; he was also my friend. And he'd not only know how this should be handled; he would make Lee's safe return his top priority and be able to spur the police into a thorough and speedy investigation. Yes, I decided as I drove the Land Rover over the Harlem River and into the Bronx, I'd place the whole matter—Lee's life and well-being, not to mention my own—into Nolan's capable hands. He'd know what to do.

With more than an hour's driving time ahead of me, I turned on the radio, scanned through channels that held little or no interest, then impatiently killed the useless and irritating squawk.

I sat behind the wheel in frustrated silence. Somehow I had to solve the puzzles of the last two days. Maybe if I resolved those, I'd also be able to figure out what had happened to my wife. But how?

Lee had always kidded me that in our previous adventures I had each time managed to successfully find a parallel between the real-life situation and a plot from a famous mystery novel. She'd even teased that had I not been such an avid mystery reader, I'd never have enjoyed any luck whatsoever as an amateur sleuth. Well, if my mystery education had helped me in the past, why couldn't it do so again?

But I had already explained to Lee that I couldn't recall any fictional story that was in any way reminiscent of this present situation. Every mystery novel I'd ever read at least had suspects, yet this case provided none. Maybe, then, I shouldn't focus so much attention on that one particular idiosyncrasy but instead see if I couldn't identify some other approach.

Free association, stream of consciousness—that's what I needed. Completely clear my mind and just see what pops out. Okay?

Okay.

So how's this supposed to work?

Be quiet. Give it time.

Nothing.

It's supposed to start slow.

Well, it's definitely living up to expectations.

Still nothing.

Sue Grafton.

Where does that get me?

Just be patient.

I'm not too good at being patient.

"A" Is for Alibi.

Ah, finally. The book's certainly one of the most expensive of the modern collectibles, commanding anywhere from eight to twelve hundred dollars.

I shook my head. That isn't much help, I thought unhappily. This isn't getting me anywhere.

And I don't need an alibi. Or maybe I do. After all, Lee is the only one who could verify my movements and whereabouts at all times.

But *"A" Is for Alibi* isn't even my favorite Kinsey Millhone story. That honor goes to *"B" Is for Burglar*—and if there's one thing I do know about this case, it's that there's not a burglar in sight.

Then try again.

Let's see. What comes to mind? John Dunning's *Booked to Die*. A police detective becomes a book dealer set in Denver. Certainly one of the most enjoyable mysteries I've ever read. But it triggers nothing.

Next.

Come on, you can't be brain dead. Thomas Berger. Get real, Berger's not a mystery writer.

John Belushi. I laughed out loud. This is bordering on the ridiculous.

Ah, but there is a connection, weird as it might sound. Everything's a "B." *"B" Is for Burglar, Booked to Die*, Berger, and Belushi.

How could that be significant?

All "B's." All bees. I nodded my head. All right, keep going. Bee what? Bee stings? Beeswax? The birds and the bees? I smiled. Bees in the bonnet? Of course, that was it. I had come up with something after all. This whole free association gambit had proved unquestionably that I had bees in my bonnet. Now that made sense.

I shrugged. So put an end to this stupidity, I decreed. I've wasted enough time on such a harebrained experiment. I reached once again for the car radio, then decided against it.

At times like this, I really regretted my pact with Lee to give up smoking. Not only had cigarettes usually calmed me down, but there had always been particular moments when I missed the habit most intensely—first thing in the morning over a cup of coffee. After a good meal. And behind the wheel. Especially then. Long stretches of boring concrete somehow always seemed more bearable with a cigarette between my lips. And, boy, could I use one now! I needed a break not only from the hypnotizing monotony of the road but also from the deadening lethargy that gripped my brain. To save Lee, I desperately needed my sharpest wits. I decided to stop at the next convenience store. I hadn't had a cigarette in months, hadn't even been around secondhand smoke in weeks until last night. Lee might protest, but surely she would understand the extreme pressure that knocked me— temporarily, of course—from the ranks of the reformed.

Without realizing it, I started to whistle. It took me a half minute to recognize the tune. "Back Home Again in Indiana."

Oh no, I groaned. Not another "B." Philip Morris, where are you?

I chose not to stop for cigarettes, after all. By the time the next mini-mart came into view, I had decided that smoking even one cigarette would somehow seem like a personal betrayal of Lee's trust. And more guilt was the last thing I needed at this particular time.

Instead, I kept my mind firmly fixed on the drive ahead.

October is one of those rare months—April is another— when New York and Connecticut really dazzle. While a few hundred miles to the north, autumn might already have soaked nature's canvas in vivid colors, here the leaves on the trees suggested only a hint of the seasonal spectacle yet to come. The farther I distanced the Land Rover from Manhattan's concrete jungle, the more frequently I glimpsed wide expanses of green lawns and manicured gardens. The outside world was lush with life and beauty, verve and vitality. Almost in spite of myself, I felt my spirits begin to rise.

The sky had darkened by the time I finally reached the outskirts of Tipton, and a few minutes later the downtown streetlamps came on in a blaze of yellow light. As I made the right-hand turn onto River Bend, it was hard to believe that it had only been yesterday morning since I had last glimpsed this well-known stretch of potholed asphalt. So much had happened in the interim—murder, ambush, kidnapping—that I certainly felt changed, and somehow I guess I expected this familiar piece of real estate to also reflect that change. But it didn't. River Bend remained a quiet cul-de-sac, with comfortable and attractive houses occupying one side of the street while on the other a narrow stretch of wooded parkland led down to the Yessula. As usual, there appeared to be little outside activity—mine is not a neighborhood routinely given over to gangs of boisterous school-age children. Fortunately, these attentive parents exerted more control over their kids. Driving down the block, I noticed in passing that several cars hugged the curb around a neighbor's house—it must be Tupperware night at the Cornwells' again—while at the end of the street a UPS delivery truck sat in abandoned silence in the middle of the turnaround.

Pulling into my driveway and easing the Land Rover to a stop in front of the closed garage door, I realized I was glad there had been no visible changes to my street. Not here. After all, this was home, and to me the word meant much more than just a house at the end of a narrow street, or a couple of lines on the outside of an envelope. Home stood for continuity, dependability, security. It was a place where the simple act of coming home never failed to delight me. And where even this particular moment, with all its worries and preoccupations, proved no exception.

With mounting excitement, I walked up the flagstoned path to the front door. I held the key ready in my hand, but, even as I aimed it at the lock, I suddenly decided that it would perhaps not be prudent to just walk in on Nolan unannounced, even if it was my own house. Instead, I rang the bell.

Bootsie's answering bark was undoubtedly the most welcome sound I'd heard in the last two days. As I listened to the approaching footsteps—both human and canine—I braced myself for Bootsie's predictable onslaught, hoping that Nolan would not be trampled in the process. But it wasn't my precious dog whom I folded gratefully into my arms a few seconds later, since it wasn't Nolan who had opened the door.

It was Lee.

CHAPTER **NINETEEN**

"Like all good magicians,
this talented author relies heavily
on
intentional misdirection
and
dazzling sleight of hand."

—Stokes Moran,
on Daniel Stashower's *Elephants in the Distance*

"*I* thought you had been kidnapped!" I blurted hoarsely while covering Lee's face with kisses and holding her tight against my chest.

"No, no, no." She laughed in my ear. "Whatever made you think that?"

But further conversation had to be forestalled when Bootsie finally succeeded in breaking out of Nolan's protective and restraining grasp, assaulting me with her furious and enthusiastic canine greeting. Acting as if she hadn't seen me in months, the frenzied Irish setter first knocked me off balance back against the door frame and then continued her conquest by tumbling me down onto the floor. In almost the same continuous blur of movement she stood over me and licked every inch of my face, her tail happily beating the air. Finally I called a halt to her antics, laughingly brushed the telltale dog spittle off my skin, and stood up.

"Where's Wee?" I asked Lee in sudden concern once I'd regained my feet. Normally the ferret stayed right at Bootsie's heels. Since the little animal was nowhere in sight, her absence gave me a momentary fright.

"She's upstairs, safely closed behind your bedroom doors," Nolan said. "Admittedly she's not too thrilled with the arrangement," he added with a laugh, "but with all the recent comings and goings around here, I just didn't want to take any chance that she might somehow get away. Have you ever considered getting her a cage?"

Having earlier registered his nearby presence in my peripheral vision, I now turned my full attention on Nolan, who stood just behind Lee and Bootsie, at the threshold to the living room. Beyond him I could see two men attired in gray business suits—both strangers to me—standing somewhat stiffly and ill at ease in front of the wall of bookshelves. I did recognize—although I could not at this moment recall his name—a uniformed UPS deliveryman who on several occasions had substituted for our regular driver. Contrary to the demeanor of the other two men, Mr. UPS lounged with apparent nonchalance against the fireplace brickfront.

"Who are these men?" I demanded, quickly returning to the fear and worry that had haunted me for the past few hours. "And what are they doing in my house?"

I shifted my gaze back and forth between Lee and Nolan. Neither immediately offered a response. "What's going on here?"

Lee smiled and took me by the hand. "Nolan will tell you all about it." She then led me into the living room, pushed me down on the sofa, snuggled up against me, and pulled my right arm up and across her shoulders. Nolan followed us in from the foyer and perched in his usual position on the recliner. Bootsie meantime took up her normal position at my feet. If only the other three men could somehow miraculously vanish, any accidental onlooker stumbling into the scene would probably conclude that here was just another Norman Rockwell depiction of domestic tranquillity at the Kyle Malachi residence.

But I knew better.

I frowned. "I don't understand any of this."

"You will, darling," Lee whispered.

"I have to apologize to you, old buddy," Nolan said, leaning into the La-Z-Boy. "Believe me, I never meant for any of this to happen, and I certainly didn't intend for things to get so out of hand."

"What are you saying, Nolan?"

"Just that I'm sorry I put you through all this." He nodded, including Lee in the expansive gesture. "I hope both of you will be able to forgive me. I had no idea things would get so complicated." He shifted his gaze toward the bookcases and glared at the two men, who still had not been introduced to me, and added, "Or so fouled up."

I shook my head. "Nolan, I don't think I'm following you. You make it sound like you're the killer."

He looked at me with just the trace of a smile on his lips and the hint of a grin behind his eyes. "That's right, old buddy. That's exactly who I am."

Lockwood picked that particularly tense and dramatic moment to saunter in from the kitchen, carrying a partially eaten sandwich in his left hand, and dangling a can of beer in the right.

"Will somebody please tell me what's going on?" I pleaded in dismay. "Nolan, I know you. You're no murderer!"

He laughed. "You got that right."

"Then are you out of your mind?" I argued, my voice rising with emotion. "Do you have any idea how unfunny this joke is?"

"It's not a joke."

"Then, what are you saying?" I tried to calm my anger.

"I killed the man," he said matter-of-factly, "but it was not murder."

"Then what was it?"

"Self-defense."

"What—?" I started.

"Self-defense," he repeated. Nolan then leaned forward in the chair and clasped his hands on his knees. "But, Kyle, why don't you just hold all your questions, and let me explain."

"I'd really appreciate that," I said, then added with a hint of sarcasm, "if you can."

"Oh, I can." He rested his head back against the cushion. He paused for a minute before he started up again.

"As you know," Nolan said, "I was over here with you on Thursday evening when you had that big blowup with Lee over Stokes Moran. And I also overheard your call to *The New York Times* announcing his death."

I shifted impatiently on the sofa. "What's that got to do with anything?" I asked irritably.

He laughed. "It's got everything to do with what you've been going through these past two days, old buddy," he said. "But please, no more questions until I finish. Okay?"

I grudgingly nodded a vow.

"I left here," Nolan continued, "sometime a little after seven, I think it was. It was dinnertime, and I wanted to get back to my house. Leave you and the little lady to sort out your own squabbles.

"I had just walked into my kitchen—hadn't even turned on the lights—when somebody suddenly jumped me from behind. Almost knocked the breath out of me. Before I knew it, a knife was at my throat and a voice in my ear was ordering me into my bedroom.

"Why the guy didn't kill me immediately, I don't know."

Nolan shook his head and laughed. "I guess that was his fatal mistake.

"Anyway, we walked almost piggyback style through the living room and into the hallway. What little light we'd had up till then had filtered in through the outside windows. But once we got into that hallway, it was virtually pitch black.

"I knew I had to try something, because if he got me into the bedroom, where there would be more light, I'd have little or no chance to come out of this thing alive. Even though I couldn't see him, I could sense his physical bulk. I could tell that he both outweighed me and towered over me. I could only hope that all my past police training—training I'd always grumbled about taking—would somehow offset his size advantage. But even if it didn't, I decided I didn't have much, if anything, to lose by making a move.

"So with the knife still scraping my throat"—here Nolan craned his head, displaying the still raw trace marks of the knife—"I elbowed him in the gut, grabbed his knife hand, and at the same time did—what's the ballet term?—a pirouette so that we were now face-to-face. I can't explain it well enough to let you know how fast this all happened. Believe me, it could only be measured in nanoseconds, that's how quick it was.

"We struggled. With me trying to wrench the knife from his one hand, he was gouging at my eyes with the other. Then we tripped and fell. Remember, still in total darkness.

"As we fell, I got all tangled up in his arms and legs. Luckily by the time we landed on the floor, the man had stopped his assault. It took me a couple of seconds to extricate myself from his grasp, get up, and turn on the hall light.

"At that point I could see why the fight had abruptly gone out of him. The life had too. An ugly-looking stiletto protruded from his chest—I guess he had fallen on it—and he was no longer breathing."

"Nolan, why didn't you just call the police?" Despite my earlier promise, I couldn't resist asking.

He smiled.

"But that's exactly what I did do."

"But not the kind of police you might think," Nolan elaborated. "And this is where I have to take you back to a time that in terms of years is really not so long ago, but for me it was a time that represented a completely different life.

"I wasn't born Nolan James, you know. That's a rather recent name for me." He smiled. "But it's one I've gotten used to and sorta like.

"I can't tell you my real name, and I promise that's the only thing I'll keep from you. Trust me when I say that if I shared that name with you, it would put you and Lee and your unborn child in too much danger, and I wouldn't want to do that, notwithstanding the last two days. I'm just too fond of you, old buddy, to ever risk that.

"And I'm not going into a lot of details. The less you know, the better.

"I'll just say that I've always tried to be honest with you. The history you know about me is true, it just was never complete." Here he smiled again, and I thought I glimpsed a tear forming in the corner of his left eye. Or maybe it was just the lighting.

"You always thought me an old bachelor, didn't you, old buddy? Well, that wasn't always the case. Believe it or not, I once had a wonderful wife. And two beautiful children. I guess we had what you'd consider the perfect American family.

"Had a great job too. Loved being a cop, loved my city. Detroit.

"But one day I stumbled on a nasty little secret, and I discovered that not all the cops on the force were as honest as I was.

"I had a choice to make. I could have become as dirty as they were, or I could try to change the way things worked. I opted for the latter.

"Lotta people came down in the sting. Lotta important people, powerful people. Police officials, politicians, government contractors. Million-dollar scandal is what it was."

He shook his head. "Don't get me wrong. I didn't do it all myself, I wasn't even the one who took the most chances or ran the greatest risks. But I suppose you could say I was the catalyst.

"I was also a witness. And a marked man."

Nolan suddenly rose to his feet, walked around behind the recliner, and propped his elbows on the chair's headrest.

"There was a leak. I was supposed to be anonymous. But these things happen. My wife and kids got blown apart by the car bomb meant for me.

"Little late." He laughed bitterly, pain and loss sharply apparent in his shaking voice. "Kinda like scraping roadkill off the highway after the buzzards have cleaned the bones. But that's when they put me in the federal witness protection program.

"After I testified, they moved me to New York. Altered my appearance a little. Even let me go back to being a cop for a while.

"Then somebody got wind I'd been ID'd. So I retired to good old Tipton with a new name.

"And a new best friend." Nolan looked at me.

"Thank you," I said.

"And this is where I've stayed for the last couple of years. Safe and sound. Until two nights ago.

"So with a dead hit man on my floor, I called my keepers"—here he swept his right arm out toward the men in the room—"and I thought they would take care of it, and that would be the end of it.

"Little did I know." Nolan walked back to the front of the

recliner and reclaimed his seat. "That's when the shit really hit the fan.

"And it was nobody's fault but my own."

"We had two immediate concerns, of course. One, get rid of the body, and two, get me out of town. Fast. Tipton wasn't safe for me anymore; there'd obviously been another leak.

"But I didn't want to run the risk of more goons showing up here, perhaps even hurting you.

"So we had to move the body. It's not easy to make a corpse disappear, not even with the assistance of the federal government." He grinned. "But then I remembered a case in lower Manhattan when I'd been a cop down there where a body had been dumped in an air shaft between buildings and had not been discovered for a coupla weeks. I talked Fredericks here"—Nolan nodded toward the taller of the gray suits—"into taking the body down there. Unfortunately one fact I had failed to remember from that first case was the body had been dumped in February, when people are not quite so prone to open their windows." He grinned again.

"But before Fredericks and Kohler"—the other gray suit?—"took the body away, we searched his pockets for information. Found driver's license and credit cards that identified my would-be executioner as Zacharias Fortunato. Confiscated all that, of course. The longer the body went undiscovered, and unidentified, the better. If we were lucky, Fortunato's employers might not send out another hit man for weeks, maybe even months. And by then, I'd be long gone.

"And that's when I made the biggest blunder of my adult life.

"Last January, while you and Lee were out in Los Angeles and I was collecting your mail—remember you told me to open anything that looked important?—Visa sent Stokes Moran a preapproved credit card application." Nolan reached into the front of his pants and pulled a wallet out of his pocket. He opened it up and retrieved a credit card, then extended it toward me. "Imagine that. A credit card for an imaginary man. All I had to do was sign the application in his name."

"How did you get this?" I asked, taking the card in my right hand.

"Lockwood returned it to me just a little while ago, along with all the rest of the fake ID's, once I had explained to him everything that had happened. They're all yours now, you can destroy them if you wish, or hang on to them as souvenirs of this little adventure."

I interrupted Nolan once again. "What ever made you sign that credit card application in the first place?" I asked. "And how come I never got any bills from them?"

"Because the card was never used," Nolan answered the second question first, "and I simply called them up and requested that they not send statements unless a payment was due." He dropped the wallet on the coffee table.

"As simple as that?" I said.

Nolan nodded. "When you're on the run like I am, you never know when you might need a new identity. And this was just too good an opportunity to pass up. If things got bad in a hurry, I could always pretend to be Stokes Moran—who I knew didn't exist—until the feds could come up with a more permanent new identity for me.

"So over the next few months, whenever I had the chances, I added more and more corroboration to my Stokes Moran portfolio, even including a fake social security card.

"I don't believe I ever really thought I'd need the stuff, mind you. It was more like having a safety net. And I felt you wouldn't mind. But of course I couldn't exactly ask your permission, old buddy, because then I would have had to tell you everything."

I frowned, shaking my head. "I understand all that, Nolan. And you're right. I would never have objected to your using

Stokes Moran's name, especially if it helped save your life. But what I don't understand is how that identification got on Fortunato's body."

"That was the biggest mistake of all," he said with a grin. "I put it there."

CHAPTER **TWENTY**

"Not until
the final page has been turned
can the reader
ever feel totally confident
that
the author's last trick
has been pulled."

—Stokes Moran,
on Ross Thomas's *The Fourth Durango*

"Why?"

Nolan shrugged. "I thought it might buy me a few extra days. Send the local cops off on a wild-goose chase for a little while at least." Here he looked at Lockwood and grinned. "Eventually, I knew, Fortunato's real identity would be established, but the longer I could delay that inevitability, the better my chances to evade the next hitter who undoubtedly would be sent."

"But it didn't work out quite the way you intended," I protested. "The cops came after me instead."

Nolan laughed. "Yeah, I know. When you called me yesterday with that news, I was virtually walking out the door. I'd already packed what little I could take with me, the feds were waiting outside, and I wasn't taking any chances by answering the phone. But when I heard your voice on the machine, I couldn't resist talking to you one last time. Then when I heard your story, old buddy, I knew I couldn't just leave you in such a predicament. I didn't believe you were ever a serious suspect"—again, he looked at Lockwood, who supplied a confirming shake of his head—"but I knew you were worried, and that wasn't fair. It was my mess, and I had to extricate you from it if I could.

"That's when other people got involved, and the whole thing really got out of hand."

"What do you mean?" I asked.

"Well, first off, I was still in shock that the body had been discovered so quickly. So I relayed your information to Agent Fredericks, who in turn contacted the U.S. attorney's office in Manhattan. They immediately dispatched one of their assistants to try to stonewall Lockwood."

"Which only made matters worse." Lockwood spoke for the first time.

"Yeah," Nolan agreed. "And it also increased the danger. We knew there had to be a leak somewhere, and if the leak had come from the U.S. attorney's Manhattan office, it meant Fortunato's employers could conceivably know of his failure and already be sending in a replacement."

"But you stayed," I said. "Weren't you running a terrible risk?"

"You solved that little problem yourself, old buddy," Nolan answered.

"Me? How did I do that?"

"By asking me to take care of your animals, of course. I could stay here at your house, out of sight and hopefully out of harm's way. It really was a perfect solution. A would-be assassin would probably never think to look so close to home, and from our vantage point here we could keep a round-the-clock watch on my place to see if anybody else showed up."

"Did anyone?"

Nolan shook his head. "Not yet, thankfully. But that's not where our next problem came from."

"What do you mean?"

"You, old buddy." He laughed. "You decided to investigate."

"But—"

"I tried to talk you out of it. Remember? Let the police handle it."

"But he wouldn't listen," Lee said.

"I couldn't just sit back and do nothing," I protested.

Nolan smiled. "Well, all in all, I have to say you did a pretty good job."

"What?" I couldn't believe my ears.

"I have to confess I missed the significance of that matchbook entirely. Of course, I was looking for other things at the time. Oh, I saw it when I went through Fortunato's pockets. But all I did was put it back where I found it, thinking it would make another nice red herring for the police. And it probably fell out onto the sidewalk when we were trying to get the body out of the car, and, of course, the bag lady picked it up. I have to admit, especially as a former cop, that I should have looked at the matchbook more closely. Like you did."

"You mean something came from that, after all?"

Nolan nodded his head. "Your interview at Tootsie's. Turns out our leak was not all that terrific at subterfuge. From what you described in your statement to Lockwood, the feds were able to identify the man almost immediately. Name's Joseph O'Bannon. Works in the records department of the Manhattan U.S. attorney's office." Nolan paused, then added, "Or I should say he did work there, up until an hour or so ago, that is, when three federal marshals placed him under arrest."

I whistled. "How was it possible to get to him so fast?"

Nolan laughed. "Seems his reputation had already preceded him. Let's just say that certain of O'Bannon's characteristics were already well known to some of his co-workers. All it took was you pointing us in the right direction, and bingo! We got him. And I could have done that Thursday night if only I'd been a little bit more perceptive."

"That's great," I said. "Does this mean you don't have to leave?"

Nolan shook his head, a sad-looking smile playing across his lips. "Unfortunately, no. I guess you'll have to break in a new neighbor, old buddy."

I was crestfallen. "But surely you can keep in touch."

"I'll do the best I can," he promised.

The conversation sounded as if it were coming to an end. But I suddenly realized I had more questions yet to be answered.

"What about Amy?" I asked.

"Coincidence," Lockwood said. "Just what I told you I didn't believe in. She was killed by another homeless person, a man who usually shared those steps with her."

I recalled a brief glimpse of another transient as Lee and I had first entered Amy's building. But he had been gone by the time we came out. I had thought nothing of his presence or later absence at the time, but had he been Amy's killer?

"Then her murder had absolutely nothing to do with this case?"

"Oh, I wouldn't say that," Lockwood said. "Seems she died fighting over a pair of Gucci loafers."

"Oh no! Not mine!"

"Yeah, that's right. Just after you left the precinct this afternoon, I talked to Detective Stebbins, who's handling the investigation. He told me the whole story. He even recovered the shoes."

"Are you sure?" It seemed I had caused Amy's death, after all.

"Yeah, he has an eyewitness. One of the building's tenants—I think. Stebbins told me it's a photographer who keeps late hours—walked out on the steps right in the middle of the attack."

"Then that means—"

He nodded. "You must have arrived while she was gone to call the police."

"And I thought I was the person the eyewitness had seen." I frowned. "But how did the matchbook get in the sock?"

Lockwood shrugged. "Who knows? Since those were her latest acquisitions, the bag lady probably just stashed it in the sock for convenience' sake. There was a bottle opener in the other sock, which was stuffed inside one of the recovered shoes."

"So it was just a complete fluke that I ever found the matchbook in the first place?"

"Yeah, another one of those unexplained coincidences nobody would ever believe," Lee said.

"But what about your disappearance from the apartment this afternoon? What was that all about?"

"If I may?" Nolan inquired of Lee. She nodded, and he continued.

"I have to give them credit, the feds were certainly trying to get you off the hook, old buddy. Not too smart, of course, the way they went about it.

"After you called last night and told me that you had inadvertently involved yourself in another homicide, I warned them that either they must somehow remove you as a potential suspect or I was going to go to the police myself.

"Anyway, I suppose some junior G-man down at headquarters got the bright idea that if the cops thought you were a target yourself, they'd stop looking at you as a possible killer."

"You don't mean—"

"Exactly. The junior G-man shot at you just to confuse the police."

"I don't believe it!" And I didn't. At first. It was so preposterous, so outrageous. Yet, I admitted on reflection, it did have the bizarre ring of truth. Wild and crazy though it sounded, the scheme seemed just plausible enough that a perhaps frustrated bureaucratic desk jockey would indeed devise it, assuming of course that he had seen one too many episodes of "The Untouchables." Eliot Ness rides again!

"Remember, I said it was a mess. When I heard what the J. Edgar wannabe had done, I put my foot down. I told the feds to bring everybody out here, and we'd make a clean breast of things once and for all. Whether they liked it or not.

"The only problem was that you were somewhere in limbo when we picked up Lee and Lockwood. You couldn't find us, and we couldn't find you. So with your rampant paranoia, you just naturally assumed—"

This time it was my turn to complete a sentence. "That Lee had been kidnapped."

Nolan nodded in agreement. "And became unnecessarily alarmed. Again, my fault."

"Whew!" I sighed, shaking my head in appreciative amazement. "Everything seems so simple now that it's been explained. So many complications, so many variations, all from such a singular act."

"And don't forget my sheer stupidity," Nolan said.

"Not to mention Kyle's bullheadedness," Lee added.

"If only you had just told us the truth right at the beginning," I posed.

Nolan grinned. "What! And have you miss out on all this fun! Why, the striptease alone was worth the price of admission."

If you say so, I thought. But I remained obstinately unconvinced.

CHAPTER **TWENTY-ONE**

"If you like your mysteries
spiced with
a little teasing
and
a lot of laughs,
you won't want to miss
this classic farce."

—Stokes Moran,
on Caroline Graham's *Murder at Madingley Grange*

"*Y*ou have to admit one thing," Lee commented after the last of our visitors had departed, "it was a comedy of errors from the start."

"You can say that again," I concurred.

"With you and me as the stooges."

"And Nolan as the straight man," I added as I headed up the stairs. "I never would have guessed that."

"Where are you going?"

"To free Wee from her forced confinement."

"Then be careful when you come back down the stairs," Lee called after me. "You know how she likes to get under your feet."

When I opened my bedroom door, Wee was waiting patiently, if somewhat unhappily, on the other side. By way of apology, I swept the little animal up in my arms and kissed her on the nose. "Hello, sweetheart," I said, rubbing my cheek against her soft, baby-fine fur, "did you miss me?" I then solved the potential problem of the stairs by depositing the ferret on my shoulder, where she remained contentedly perched until I returned to the living room and collapsed onto the sofa. As soon as my shoulder hit the backrest, Wee scampered away, down and off the sofa, and headed toward the kitchen, where she would presumably find her food dish brimming with culinary delectables. I guessed that Lee and Bootsie had also retreated into the kitchen—since they were nowhere else in sight—so, rather than sit in splendid isolation, I opted to join the rest of my family.

"I see everybody's eating," I said. And it was true. Lee sat at the table, a cup of strawberry yogurt and a bag of pretzels open in front of her, while Bootsie and Wee were busily occupied over their own individual bowls. With all the other members of my happy little household stuffing their faces, I suddenly realized that I hadn't eaten a morsel of food since breakfast.

"How do you feel," Lee asked amid spoonfuls, "now that all the excitement is over?"

"Relieved."

"Is that all you have to say? Just that you're relieved?"

"What else would you have me say?"

"Oh, I don't know." She munched on a pretzel. "Maybe grateful, or happy or sad, or tired?"

"Those too," I said with a smile.

Lee and I sat in companionable silence. Before he left, Nolan had officially introduced me to agents Fredericks and Kohler, and to Tim Luster as well, the substitute UPS deliveryman, who it turned out was not a UPS driver at all but a regular member of Nolan's protection team.

"Very good cover," I told Nolan as we stood just inside the front door and watched Luster walk to his truck.

"Yeah, and he gets to keep the tips too."

We both laughed.

Then Lockwood approached, his hand outstretched. "I hope there's no hard feelings, Mr. Malachi. I didn't mean to give you such a hard time."

"Think nothing of it," I said, accepting his handshake, "you were just doing your job."

"Oh, before I forget it." He reached inside his jacket. "Here's your money clip. I never meant to keep it in the first place. You just forgot to take it back."

"Thank you," I said, grateful to have my money and identification back in my own hands.

"I guess I'll say good night then."

Nolan and I each nodded at Lockwood as he edged through the door and slipped outside. Since Lee had opted not to join the male exodus into the foyer, Lockwood's departure now left only Nolan and me standing awkwardly alone. Neither one of us said anything for a full minute.

"Tall drink of water, isn't he?" Nolan commented, finally breaking the silence, then cleared his throat and said, "Well, old buddy, I suppose this is good-bye. At least for now."

"You will keep in touch, won't you? The baby will be here in about two months."

He smiled. "I'll call at Christmas. The kid'll be here by then, right?"

I nodded. "Delivery is scheduled for the week before. December eighteenth."

He clasped my right arm just below the elbow in both his hands. "I never had a better neighbor."

"Neither did I."

"I'm going to miss you."

"Me too."

"Oh, you'll forget all about me as soon as some pretty college coed moves in next door."

I laughed. "I seriously doubt it."

"Well, they're waiting for me."

"Yeah."

Abruptly Nolan threw his arms around my shoulders in a bearlike hug. I squeezed back. Then he broke the embrace and darted toward a black sedan.

"Wait!" I shouted. "Nolan, come back for a minute." By the time Nolan had returned to the door, I'd had the opportunity to rush into the living room and back.

"I think this rightfully belongs to you." I held out the advance copy of my book—*Alias Stokes Moran.* "Don't you think?"

We both laughed at the joke. "Not without an autograph, though," Nolan insisted.

Nolan handed me a pen, and I thought what to say. There was so much I could say, so much that had remained unsaid. How I treasured his friendship. How much I had appreciated all the little kindnesses he'd performed for me over the years. How much I was going to miss him. Finally, I decided simplest was best. "For the real Stokes Moran," I wrote. "With all my love."

Nolan took back his pen and read what I had written. "Thanks," he said, then added one final comment.

I nodded, and he turned and walked away. I closed the door before he had a chance to look back.

His parting words still echoed in my ears. "Never forget, old buddy. Everybody has a secret.

"Everybody."

"How do you feel about Stokes Moran now?" Lee asked after a long silence.

I smiled. "I have to admit that I'm not jealous of him anymore. I think all those feelings got exorcised out of me the last couple of days."

"Good," she said. "Then he rises from the dead, after all."

"We already agreed he would, even before all this. Remember?"

Lee reached across the table and affectionately patted my hand. "I wanted to make sure you hadn't changed your mind." Then, with just a hint of sarcasm, she added pointedly, "Again."

"No way. As far as I'm concerned Stokes Moran is here to stay."

"I'm happy to have him back," she said, scraping the last vestige of the yogurt from the cup.

"So am I." Then abruptly changing the subject, I asked, "How would you like some spaghetti?"

Lee looked at me in amazement. "You're offering to cook?"

"Sure, why not? This is a red-letter day."

"What kind of sauce are you going to make?" Lee said eagerly, joining me at the sink.

"How about primavera?"

She squinted up her nose in distaste. "Why don't you let me make the sauce."

With Lee's current penchant for inedible combinations, I doubted the wisdom of such a move, but she was already scouring the shelves for ingredients. I decided to give her her head. After all, whatever she concocted wouldn't exactly kill us. I hoped.

"You know," I said, carefully carrying the water-filled pan over to the stovetop, "I still feel guilty about Amy. If it hadn't been for me, she'd still be alive."

"You don't know that." Lee's voice was somewhat muffled, her head buried deep in the freezer.

"Well, my shoes caused the fight."

"If it hadn't been your shoes," Lee said, now clear of the refrigerator and holding a two-pound package of frozen hamburger in her hand, "it would have been something else. Maybe not yesterday, possibly tomorrow, or next week. People who live on the streets are in constant danger."

"Lee, it's going to take forever for that meat to thaw."

"Not if I stick it in the microwave," she said, then followed her words with a matching action.

I frowned. "You know how I hate defrosting meat in the microwave."

She nodded. "Yeah, yeah, I know. You're afraid you'll get food poisoning. Well, get over it," she said. "I'm making the sauce."

I ripped open a fifteen-ounce container of angel hair pasta, prepared to dunk it in the pan as soon as the water started to boil.

"Open another one," Lee instructed.

"What?"

"That's not enough."

"Lee, we'll be overrun with spaghetti."

"Don't worry, it'll get eaten."

I was tempted to say that's just what I'm afraid of, but I kept my mouth diplomatically shut. Lee reached into the cabinet, pulled another container of spaghetti off the shelf, and handed it to me. "Open it."

I sighed, then did as she instructed.

"You know," she said, folding her arms across her chest while waiting for the microwave to finish its run, "this was one mystery you didn't solve by calling on your encyclopedic knowledge of famous mystery novels."

I smiled. "I'm not so sure about that."

"What!" Lee dropped her hands dramatically to her sides. "Come on, now. Are you trying to tell me you had it figured out before Nolan confessed?"

"Maybe."

"Bull." The bell went off, and she opened the microwave and retrieved the zapped meat. "Don't give me that. I watched you. You were as astonished by his story as I had been."

I nodded my head. "You're right, I was."

"Then what are you trying to say?"

"While I was driving up here this afternoon," I explained while stirring the now limp pasta with a wooden ladle, "I tried a little free association."

"Free association?"

"You know, stream of consciousness."

She frowned, pulling six jars off the spice rack. "I know what it is, Kyle. I'm not a child, after all. I just don't understand what free association has to do with anything."

"Well, since this case didn't have any suspects, and I hadn't really gotten anywhere, and I was worried you'd been kidnapped—"

"Spit it out," she interrupted, liberally sprinkling oregano onto the hamburger with one hand, while kneading the meat with the other.

"I tried to clear my brain and see if anything popped out."

Lee laughed. "And did it?" she asked, now dumping garlic salt and onion powder into the mix, followed in quick order by basil, rosemary, and black pepper.

"Yeah, it was really interesting, but of course at the time I didn't know what it meant."

"Oho!" Both her hands disappeared into the mixture. "Now you're claiming you solved the case through free association."

"No, I'm claiming nothing of the kind."

"Well, are you going to tell me what you came up with?" she asked, wiping her hands on a dish towel and walking over to the refrigerator. "Or do you want me to torture it out of you?"

I grinned. "You don't have to do that, I'll tell you."

She returned to the counter with a can of beer. "Well?"

"What do 'B' Is for Burglar, Booked to Die, Thomas Berger, John Belushi, and "Back Home Again in Indiana" suggest to you?"

She snapped the pull tab. "You mean besides the obvious alliteration of 'B's'?"

"Yes."

Lee squinted her eyes in mock concentration. "I give up. I have no idea."

"Neighbors," I announced with pride.

Lee looked at me as if I'd just arrived from the "Outer Limits." "So?"

"Don't you get it? My subconscious mind was trying to give me the solution, only I wasn't smart enough to understand."

"Neighbors, huh?" She shrugged. "I'm sorry. I still don't get it. I think you're making the whole thing up."

"You think I'd really do that?" I asked with hurt pride.

"Yes," she answered adamantly, "in order to try to make me think you're cleverer than you are."

"Well, just for that I'm not going to explain the connection."

"Good." Lee lifted the can to her mouth and downed a hefty swig.

"But any intelligent person will be able to figure it out."

"I'm not even going to try," she said, pouring the rest of the beer into the hamburger mixture.

"Lee, what are you doing?" I asked, appalled.

"I'm making a sauce we'll never forget."

With my stomach groaning with anticipatory contractions, I didn't doubt that for a moment.

CHAPTER **TWENTY-TWO**

"How the arrival
on the scene
of a newborn heir
may further complicate
the wacky lives
of these lovable lunatics
is anyone's guess."

—Stokes Moran,
on Charlotte MacLeod's *The Recycled Citizen*

"*K*yle, stop here!"

"But, Lee, this is a tow-away zone."

"I don't care!" she screamed. "Get me into that hospital now!"

Less than an hour later, after being rushed through the Tipton Women's Clinic emergency admissions and then sped directly into the delivery room, Lee gave birth to our first child, a healthy and intact eight-pound-two-ounce baby boy.

A few minutes after that, I got to hold him in my arms for the first time, standing beside Lee's bed and looking down into my wife's radiant and smiling face, the baby cooing contentedly in his father's embrace.

"He's got your nose," I told her.

She laughed. "Oh, I hope not."

"Why? I happen to think your nose is awfully cute." For added emphasis, I leaned down and planted a kiss on the tip of her nose, then repeated the gesture on the baby.

"We have to get him into the nursery," the attending nurse said, taking him from my arms.

"Can't we keep him a little while longer?" I implored.

"Sorry, both mother and child need their rest." The nurse allowed Lee one last kiss to the baby's cheek. As she swept toward the door, the nurse warned over her shoulder, "And, papa, no more than two more minutes. You've got to leave too."

Suddenly, in the wake of their departure, the hospital room seemed once again drab and sterile. I smiled down at my wife.

"You did good," I said.

She laughed. "So did you."

"He's so beautiful."

"Yes."

"And sweet. He didn't cry the entire time I held him, just gurgled once or twice."

"That's because he knew it was his father who was holding him."

I laughed. "So that's what it was. Or are you already psyching me up for all those late-night feedings yet to come? I'm no pushover, you know."

She smiled lazily. "If you say so."

"Well, I'm not!" I pretended outrage.

Lee yawned. "Have you given any more thought to what we're going to name him?"

"I've got a couple of ideas, but we can discuss them tomorrow."

"The baby needs a name, Kyle."

"I know, but for right now he's listed as Baby Boy Malachi on his wristband. I saw it. The strip was so cute wrapped around his tiny little arm."

Lee's brow creased into a light frown. "Baby Boy Malachi is not what I would call a proper name for our child."

"It'll do until tomorrow." I leaned down and nuzzled my lips against Lee's ear.

"Tomorrow's already here," she murmured sleepily. "It's almost dawn."

I gently caressed her left hand, holding it between my fingers while I quietly eased away from the bed, palm touching palm until by my increasing distance the hand dropped peacefully on top of the bedcovers.

"Kyle"—Lee suddenly startled awake—"you know I hate an unresolved mystery. We've got to agree on the baby's name."

Standing in the doorway, I turned to face the bed and whispered, "Tomorrow."

She frowned. "All right, if you insist. But now that I've presented you with a son, do you think you could answer me one question?"

I smiled. "Anything."

"Good," she said triumphantly. "Then explain the 'B's.' That riddle has been torturing me for nearly two months."

"Okay. As I told you, the common link was neighbors." I then lifted my right hand and counted off the points. "In both *'B' Is for Burglar* and *Booked to Die,* neighbors figure prominently in the plots. Thomas Berger wrote a novel called *Neighbors.* And John Belushi starred in the film of the same title. So all of those 'B's' were just my subconscious nudging me in Nolan's direction. Satisfied?"

"All right, it does seem to make sense, in a Kyle Malachi kind of way," she acknowledged, then added as a reminder, "but that still leaves the song. You didn't mention it."

I shrugged. "'Back Home Again in Indiana' is played every year at the Indianapolis 500. It's a time-honored tradition."

"So?" she asked skeptically. I noticed that Lee's wedding ring suddenly sparkled against the white sheets, capturing the light from the hallway.

"Who do you think sings it?"

She shook her head. "I haven't a clue."

"Jim Nabors."

The last thing I glimpsed as the door closed soundlessly behind me was Lee's bed pillow, fired like a missile, flying straight toward my head.

As I walked—hell, floated—down that antiseptic corridor, I couldn't have been more happy, more deliriously cheerful. Here I was, at forty-one years of age (I'd had a birthday in mid-November)—it was only four days until Christmas—Lee had missed her due date by three excruciatingly frustrating days—a father for the first time. I felt reborn, energized, a kid myself. I was a new man, with a new family. I decided at that moment that I'd become a new person as well. With the addition of a new boarder, the house in Tipton would just be too small. It was time to move. Lee and I had missed Nolan even more than we'd expected, so the cul-de-sac didn't seem quite as friendly as before. I still had to wait for his call. Christmas, he'd said. I'd tell him about the move. I never wanted to lose touch with him, so I had four days to find a new address. I'd have to talk it over with Lee, of course. But somehow, Indiana felt like home. Maybe the song had subconsciously put the idea in my mind, but it felt right. My grandmother lived there, and she was past eighty. She wouldn't be around much longer. And of course, she needed to meet her new great-grandchild. So when Nolan called, I'd just give him my grandmother's address and telephone number. He could always reach me through her, and that would take the immediate pressure off trying to find a new place quickly.

But what would my sudden decision mean for the future of Stokes Moran?

Stokes Moran would retire. At least for a while, maybe forever. Now was a time for family, for friends and neighbors, for real life. No more hiding behind books or words. If my novel sold, fine. If not, also fine. I was determined to withdraw from public life. As of this moment, without further explanation. I knew Lee would offer no objection. She had been responsible for everything I had in my life now, anyway.

As the electronic exit doors parted at my approach, I felt there wasn't anything I couldn't master, nothing I couldn't handle.

But my ebullience didn't last long; as a matter of fact, it didn't even make it to the curb. You see, the Land Rover was not where I had left it. On an otherwise perfect evening, Lee's parking genie had finally returned to the bottle.

The car had been towed.

ABOUT THE AUTHOR

Neil McGaughey is the author of three previous Stokes Moran mystery novels, all published by Scribner. A full-time writer as well as a nationally known critic, he lives in rural Mississippi, where he is currently at work on a new mystery series set in historic Natchez-Under-the-Hill, the city where he was born.